The Story of Robert Bruce

The Story of Robert Bruce

by

Jeanie Lang

GET ALL OF THE 'HISTORY SHAPERS' BOOKS
The Story of...

David Livingstone
H. M. Stanley
Abraham Lincoln
Sir Francis Drake
Sir Walter Raleigh
Columbus

Robert Bruce
General Gordon
Lord Clive
Captain Cook
Nelson
Lord Roberts

Chalmers of New
Guinea
Bishop Patteson
Joan of Arc
Napoleon
Cromwell

PLEASE NOTE

In this series, you will read about historical figures who displayed courage, bravery, self-sacrifice, and many other admirable traits. Their stories remind us that many people in history took bold actions and made tough choices. Yet, even those who achieved great things sometimes held ideas or pursued goals that were not beneficial to everyone. History is full of complex individuals—parts of their lives inspire us to be brave and stand up for what is right, while other parts remind us to consider the unintended consequences of our actions.

As you explore these biographies, we invite you to reflect on the qualities that enabled these figures to achieve greatness and the lessons we can learn from their mistakes. Maybe you too can become a History Shaper—someone who learns from the past and helps to make our world a better place for everyone.

Contents

Dow the War Between England and Scotland Began

"Rule Britannia! Britannia rules the waves!
Britons never, never, never will be slaves!"

Do you know that song, you English boys and girls? And do you ever think, when you hear it, that not so very many hundreds of years ago there was no such kingdom as the kingdom of Great Britain? Or do you remember that before the country of Britain became the kingdom of Great Britain, Scotland had to fight for her freedom, and, with the blood of her people, win it from the king who ruled over England?

This is the story of how Scotland fought and won. And before we begin the story of Robert the Bruce, who led Scotland safely through those evil days, we must first learn something about how the war between England and Scotland began.

For nearly seven centuries the English and Scottish kings had quarrelled over certain pieces of land. These were mostly in the "Debateable Land," as it is still called, that lies on either side of the Tweed and the Cheviots, and where still, in many parts, only the wail of the curlews and the tinkle of mountain burns break the stillness of the lonely hill and moorland.

Because England was a much richer land than Scotland, and because its people had ceased to be savage long before the people of the north land, each succeeding king of England also thought that the Scottish king should be his "man"—that is, that he should own him to be his overlord and master.

In the thirteenth century a king called Edward I. sat on the English throne.

If you, who read this story, should be an English girl or boy, you will probably have learned that Edward I. was one of the wisest and bravest kings that England ever knew.

But should you be a Scottish girl or boy, it is more likely that you may believe that Edward I. of England was one of the most cruel, most greedy, and most unjust kings that ever wore a crown.

Had we lived in Scotland in the days of Wallace and of Bruce, it must have been impossible to think anything else. We must have hated the English as the Boers hated the British a short time ago; as the Japanese hated the Russians; as one nation has, from the beginning of time, always hated the nation with which it was at war. And we must have hated the king who ruled England just as much as English boys and girls then, and English men and women, hated the man they called "The Wicked Wallace."

But now that we Scotch and English are one nation

under one king, we are able to look back and see that Edward I. was truly a very great king and a very wise one, and that he was one of the strongest men that ever held the English sceptre. Far, far ahead of his own time he looked, and saw how good a thing it would be to have, instead of four countries always at war, one great kingdom, the Great Britain of to-day, in which should reign peace and prosperity.

But instead of bringing peace to his own country and to Scotland, it was Edward who brought about the war which ended in Scotland gaining her freedom.

For the lands held by the English kings in France they rendered homage to the French king.

For those lands held by them in England the Scottish kings did the same to the English king.

But in England the English king, and in Scotland the Scottish king, owned no master.

In England the King of Scotland was on the same footing as the English barons, and was ready to fight against foreign kings for the King of England if need arose.

Edward I. had not long come to the throne before he began to claim more than merely his allegiance for his English lands from Alexander of Scotland.

At Westminster, in 1278, Alexander did homage for the lands he held in England—*"saving my own kingdom."*

The Bishop of Norwich interrupted him. "And saving the right of my lord, King Edward, to homage for your kingdom," said the bishop.

"I own my kingdom direct from God," proudly answered the Scottish king.

On a stormy night in March 1286, Alexander III. met his death by falling over a steep cliff on the Fife coast. His two sons died before him. His daughter, the Queen of Norway, was also dead.

And Scotland was left with no one to rule her but a motherless baby girl of three, the Princess Margaret, whose father was king of the land that in Scotland they called "Noroway owre the faem."

Edward of England lost no time in making up his mind what he had best do now, to gain Scotland for himself and for future kings of England. He arranged a marriage between the little queen and his son Edward, Prince of Wales, a boy only fourteen years old.

The marriage must take place in England, he said, and when Princess Margaret was six years old, he sent what was then called "a great ship" from Yarmouth to Norway to fetch the little bride.

It was like a ship in a fairy tale, richly furnished, and loaded with all the sweetmeats and good things that the wise English king knew that little girls liked. There were sugar—then thought a rare and delicious thing in England—walnuts, figs, and raisins, and 28 lbs. of gingerbread.

But the ship came home without her.

It was on a Norwegian ship that, a few months later,

she left her snowy hills, and blue fjords, and great pine forests, and sailed away to Scotland to be its queen.

But she never got further than the bleak Orkney Islands.

Just when the land over which she was to reign was seen, a faint blue line in the south, the little maid sickened and died.

It was a sad ship that sailed again across the sea, and took home a little dead queen to lie in her own north land.

She had reigned four years, six months, and seven days.

John Balliol

As soon as news came from the Orkneys that the Maid of Norway was dead, there were many men who claimed for themselves the Scottish crown.

In all there were thirteen "competitors," as they were called, as if it were a game, or races.

The two whose claims seemed the strongest were John Balliol and Robert Bruce, grandfather of Robert the Bruce, both descendants of William the Lion, grandfather of the late king. Balliol was the great-grandson of David, Earl of Huntingdon, younger brother of William the Lion; Bruce was the grandson of the same man. But Balliol was descended from Earl David's eldest daughter, and Bruce from a younger one.

Edward of England then took a bold step. He invited the Scottish nobles and clergy, and all who laid claim to the crown, to meet him at Norham, a castle past which the silver Tweed runs between wooded banks, dividing England from Scotland.

At Norham, said Edward, he would decide for the Scottish nation who was the right man to reign over them.

The meeting took place on May 10th, 1291, and Edward made his power the more felt by the kingless people of

Scotland because of his noble escort of knights and barons in glittering armour.

"I come as your lord," at once he told the Scottish nobles. "Unless you grant that I am Lord Paramount, I will not help you."

The Scots wisely answered—

"We have no king. How can we say if our king, when we have one, will bow to you as his overlord?"

Then said Edward, in a rage—

"By Saint Edward, whose crown I wear, I will maintain my just right, or die in the cause!"

Thus it was that Scotland's fight for freedom began. Edward unjustly claimed the overlordship as his right, and all true-hearted Scotsmen denied him their homage.

Yet, at this time, the nobles who longed to wear the crown of Scotland thought second of their country, and first of themselves.

When Edward made it a condition that the man whom he, as umpire, made king must own him as master, there was not one of those who claimed the crown who did not give in to his demands.

In November 1292, in the great hall of Berwick Castle— which is now a railway station through which the trains rush which bring you from England to Scotland—Edward held a great assembly of English and Scottish nobles.

"Can you divide the kingdom of Scotland and its revenues?" Edward asked the assembly.

"No," was the answer.

"Then," said he, "as it cannot be shared between Bruce and Balliol, I appoint John Balliol, as having the stronger claim, to be your king."

John Balliol swore that he would be a faithful vassal to the King of England, his "Lord Superior." At Scone, near Perth, he was crowned on the "Stone of Destiny," upon which had never sat a more unkingly king.

The Scots called their new king the "Toom Tabard," or empty coat, so little of a man did they think him.

"We do not want this man to reign over us," they angrily said.

"But," says an old chronicler, "he, as a simple creature, opened not his mouth, fearing the frenzied wildness of that people, lest they should starve him, or shut him up in prison. So dwelt he with them a year, as a lamb among wolves."

In England, and by King Edward, Balliol was as little respected as he was in Scotland; Edward treated him not as a monarch, but as a servant whom he scorned. He heaped insults upon him, and tried by every means in his power to make Balliol repent that he had ever claimed the crown.

It was all part of Edward's scheme to win Scotland for himself.

"When I have goaded this worm into turning," he planned, "and into rebelling against me, I shall then punish him and his followers by taking his country and his crown for myself."

And presently it fell out as Edward had schemed.

The worm was provoked into turning. Balliol leagued with France against England, and defied Edward by invading the counties of Northumberland and Cumberland.

But Balliol had no loyal subjects to back him up. His people despised him. His nobles were jealous of him; many of them he had offended.

When Edward heard that Balliol had laid waste with his rabble army two English counties, his wrath was great.

"Has the fool done this folly?" he cried. "If he will not come to us, we will come to him."

With a fleet of ships, and with an army of 30,000 foot soldiers and 50,000 horsemen, he went to Berwick-on-Tweed, and besieged it by land and by sea.

Berwick was then the greatest seaport town in Scotland, the home of rich Flemish merchants who exported wool, skins, hides, and salt fish, and imported cargoes of wine, spiceries, and corn.

Its gallant garrison defied King Edward. From behind the wooden stockade, which was its only rampart, they shouted and sang mocking verses that made Edward still more furiously angry.

With the loss of only one knight, the stockade was stormed. Nearly 8000 of the citizens were slain, and a handful of brave Flemish merchants who held out in the Town Hall when all others were forced to surrender, were burned alive in it. Edward let his soldiers sack, and plunder, and pillage, and butcher wholesale men, women, and children.

"As leaves in the autumn the Scots fell," says a chronicler, and for days the Tweed ran red across the bar into the grey North Sea, carrying the dead with it.

It was only when a procession of priests bore into Edward's presence the holiest things of their Church, and begged for mercy, that the angry king made the slayers sheathe their swords.

Berwick's greatness was gone for ever. From that time it sank into a little seaport town.

The king who had dreamed of a Great Britain over which he ruled in peace and prosperity, had done the worst possible thing to make his dream a reality.

In his rage he had grown cruel, and it was a cruelty which the Scottish people never forgot or forgave.

A few weeks later the Scots brutally avenged themselves. At Corbridge, in Northumberland, they set fire to the schools and burned to death 200 "little clerks," as the schoolboys then were called.

Before he left Berwick, Edward had a deep fosse, or ditch, dug round the town, and a high wall built. Now that Berwick belonged to him, he meant that proper care should be taken of it, and so good were his fortifications that you may see parts of the "Edwardian Wall" standing at Berwick to this day. They say that he was so keen that the work should be quickly done, that he himself wheeled a barrow for the builders.

Victories at Dunbar and other places followed that at Berwick, and Edward marched in triumph through Scotland, claiming and getting the submission of the Scottish nobles. "Ragman's Roll" is the name of the document they signed, promising to be Edward's vassals, and very poor beggar-men they sound.

This done Edward returned to England, taking with him everything that it was possible to take in the way of royal plunder.

Amongst other things were the Stone of Destiny, and the Holy Rood. It was from this Holy Rood, said to be a piece of the Cross upon which Christ was crucified, that Holyrood Palace takes its name.

The Stone of Destiny belonged to the Scots from the very earliest days when they, it was said, sailed to Ireland across the sea from Spain. Many tales were told of it. One was that it was the stone upon which Jacob's head rested when he dreamed of angels going up and down to heaven.

On that stone the kings of Scotland had always been crowned, and now that England and Scotland are at war no more, those who reign over Great Britain still are crowned on the Stone of Destiny that stands in Westminster Abbey.

Chief amongst those who had helped to make Edward master of Scotland was Robert Bruce, called Le Vieil, son of that Bruce, now dead, who had claimed the crown when it was given to Balliol, and father of Robert the Bruce.

After the battle of Dunbar he came to King Edward and reminded him that it was now his turn to be king. Not only was he the nearest heir to the throne, but in days when Alexander III. had no children, he had promised Robert

Bruce, Lord of Annandale, his friend and cousin, that he should succeed him.

"Have we nothing else to do but to win kingdoms for thee?" was Edward's scornful answer.

So did Edward try to humble one of the most powerful nobles in Scotland.

King "Toom Tabard" he humbled in yet another way.

Stripped of his kingly ornaments, and with a white wand, such as penitents carried, in his hand, Balliol humbly gave up to Edward all his rights to the kingdom of Scotland. For three years he was imprisoned in London, and was then allowed to go to his estates in France, where he died thirteen years later.

Scotland was once again without a king, and was in even worse case than when its sovereign was a little girl, far across the sea.

Its castles were in the hands of English governors, who took from the Scots any property they took a fancy to. English soldiers were allowed to rob, beat, and even kill the Scots, their wives, their daughters, and their little children, without punishment.

In the years that followed Edward's triumph, had it not been for William Wallace, one of the truest patriots and greatest heroes that ever lived, the freedom of Scotland might have been lost for ever.

From 1297 until 1305 Wallace waged war against England, at first winning battles against heavy odds.

In 1305, through the treachery of a Scottish nobleman, he was betrayed to the English and brought to London.

By the king's command he was drawn on a hurdle from Westminster to the Tower, and from the Tower to Smithfield, and there he was hanged, disembowelled, and beheaded.

His limbs were sent to Newcastle, Berwickon-Tweed, Stirling, and Perth, to be exhibited there as parts of a traitor to the English king. His head was stuck on London Bridge, for the sea-birds that come up the Thames with the tide to peck at, and for sun and wind, snow and rain, to beat upon.

For fifteen years Edward I. had struggled with Scotland. When he rode across London Bridge and looked at the head of his enemy, Wallace, bleaching there, he must proudly have thought that the fight was over at last, and that he had won. He was overlord of Scotland—king in all but name.

Little he knew that in his own court, perhaps even in the train of knights who rode with him, there was one who, in six short months, was to defy the victorious king, and win for Scotland a freedom that she was never more to lose.

Robert the Bruce and the Red Comyn

You have read that the two "competitors" who had the strongest claim to the Scottish crown were John Balliol and Robert Bruce.

Robert Bruce, Lord of Annandale, was an old man while all these disputes took place.

In 1295, at the age of eighty-five, he died at his castle of Lochmaben in Dumfriesshire. His son, known as Bruce *Le Viel*, Earl of Carrick, although he had fought bravely against the Saracens in the Crusades, was a weak man, who liked better to stay peaceably in his English home than to fight for a crown which he might possibly never win.

"Have we nothing else to do but to win kingdoms for thee?" Edward I. had asked him in scorn, and Bruce *Le Viel* never put forward another claim.

When his eldest son, Robert, was seventeen, he gave up to him the earldom of Carrick, which had come to him through his wife, and until his death in 1304 he spent most of his time peacefully in England, leaving his sons to do battle for his Scottish property and the Scottish crown if they chose.

At Writtle Manor in Essex, an estate of his father's, Robert the Bruce was born on July 11, 1274.

His father's ancestors were of the noblest chivalry of France. De Brus, a Norman baron, who took his name from the lands of Breaux, in Normandy, came over with the Conqueror. Bruce's mother, daughter of the Earl of Carrick, was descended from the fighting Celtic chiefs of Galloway.

The Bruce boys, Robert, Edward, Thomas, Alexander, and Nigel, were brought up in England, and educated as English knights.

They must have grown up to hate Balliol, who had got the crown which their grandfather had claimed, and which King Alexander had promised that a Bruce should wear.

Still more must they have hated Balliol when he seized their father's lands in Annandale, and gave them to his own friend, John Comyn; at the same time taking from Robert, the young Earl of Carrick, the earldom which his father had given to him only a short while before. And Robert the Bruce, who was a strong man, and feared no one, must have scorned the Toom Tabard, who, although he wore the crown of Scotland, yet allowed the English king to order him about as a big boy orders his fag at school.

Yet, while he was a lad, and even when he was a man, at first we cannot find that Bruce had any great love for the land for which he was later to fight so nobly. He would have loved to be a king—what boy would not? But it was only of the crown of Scotland that he dreamed, and not of Scotland's freedom.

Historians in our own days say hard things of him, because sometimes he fought for Edward of England, sometimes against him just as it suited him best, so they say.

They may be right, yet Bruce was placed in very much the same position as the boy whose parents are Scotch, but who has been born in England, educated at an English public school, and at Oxford or Cambridge, and who is asked to play in the English XV. against Scotland.

And so Bruce played for England, and against the very land of which he wished to be king, as his father and grandfather had wished before him.

Of the two older Bruces Edward had always felt fairly sure. But the young Earl of Carrick, the tall, strong, handsome youth, who seemed to have no fear, and who bore himself so proudly, kept him anxious.

He did all he could to bind Robert the Bruce to him. For his services he praised and rewarded him. In 1296 he spoke of "the great esteem he" (Edward) had "for the good service of Robert de Bruys, Earl of Carrick." In the very next year he "feared for the faithlessness and inconstancy of Sir Robert de Bruys." And Bruce gave him reason to fear, by joining, for a short time, the side of Wallace. In 1298, when Edward came to Scotland to overthrow Wallace, Bruce burned down the castle of Ayr, lest Edward should take it, and retreated into the wilds of Carrick, whither he knew that an English army could not follow him.

For this Edward punished him by marching through Annandale, taking the Bruces' castle of Lochmaben, and wasting their estates.

A few weeks later, Robert the Bruce was again fighting under the English banner. But in 1299 we find him trying to drive out the English garrison placed by Edward in the castle of Lochmaben. Once more, in 1304, he changed sides. He was in charge of the English guns which battered against Stirling Castle, and which were to put an end to Wallace's struggle for freedom.

Perhaps it was at Smithfield, where, on an August day in 1305, he saw Wallace martyred for his country, that the heart of Bruce changed in its feelings to Scotland.

But of that we do not know.

There is an old story that, after one of the battles that Robert the Bruce had helped to fight and win for England, he sat down to eat with his hands still stained with the blood of the Scots he had slain. "Look at the Scotchman eating his own blood," said one English soldier to another. And Bruce was filled with shame, because he knew that what the man said was true.

Bruce's hatred to Balliol he had handed on to Balliol's nephew, John Comyn, called, from his red hair, "the Red

Comyn." Comyn was the son of one of the other claimants to the crown, and his mother was a sister of John Balliol.

More than once Comyn had defied King Edward, and he was always ready to pick a quarrel with Bruce.

In 1299, at the sleepy little town of Peebles, on the Tweed, there was held an election of guardians for Scotland. The guardians chosen were Robert the Bruce, Bishop Lamberton, and the Red Comyn.

During the council meeting of the Scottish nobles who made the choice, hot words passed between Bruce and the Red Comyn.

A chronicler tells us that Sir John Comyn "leaped on Robert Bruce, Earl of Carrick, and took him by the throat," and that John Corny, Earl of Buchan (Sir John's uncle), leaped on William Lamberton, Bishop of St. Andrews, "and they held them fast until the Steward and others went and stopped the scuffle."

In January 1306 Robert the Bruce was at Edward's court in London, one of the finest-looking of the noble knights there.

Edward must have felt about him rather as does a man who has tamed a lion, and who is never quite certain whether it will not again one day turn upon him and kill him. Yet there seemed no reason for mistrusting the lion, who had fought for him so bravely, and who for some years had served him so well.

But from Scotland there came bad news for King

Edward. The Red Comyn wrote and confessed that he and Robert the Bruce had been plotting together.

To Comyn, Bruce had said: "Give me your lands, and I will help you to win the crown for yourself; or take my lands, and help to make me king."

Comyn had agreed to take Bruce's estates, and to help him to win the crown, and had solemnly sworn to tell no one of their compact.

But not even kings or bishops in those days thought it wicked to break their oaths or mean to break their promises.

The Comyn saw a fine chance of avenging himself on his old enemy the Bruce, and told Edward the whole tale.

Edward promised to reward Comyn, and, in a great rage, sent for Bruce.

To all the king's questions and accusations Bruce answered so wisely and so pleasantly that the king's rage was softened. Until he got more news from Scotland he decided to do nothing, but forbade Bruce to leave the court without his leave.

One night, as the king and some of his lords sat over their wine, the king told the lords that he did not mean to delay any longer, but was going to have Robert the Bruce put to death on the morrow.

The Earl of Gloucester, a cousin of the Bruce, heard this. To Bruce's house he sent a trusty messenger with twelve silver pennies and a pair of spurs.

"My lord sends these to you," said the man, "in return for what he, on his side, got from you yesterday."

Bruce guessed rightly that his cousin's message meant that he must fly. He gave the money to the messenger, sent his thanks to the earl, and got ready to start for the north.

It was bitter winter weather. The ground was white with snow, and they say that Bruce had his horse, and the horses of his secretary and groom who rode with him, shod with the wrong ends of the shoes foremost, to trick his pursuers.

But, however they may have been shod, the horses did their journey well. In fifteen days from the start they were safely over the Border.

In the wild moorland country of the Western Marches they met a man plodding along on foot.

From his dress, and from the way he walked, they took him to be a Scot.

"Whence come ye?" asked Bruce, "and whither do ye go?"

The man began to tell lying tales, and the Bruce had him searched. Letters from Comyn to the king, advising that Robert the Bruce should at once be put to death, were found on him. Without more ado the messenger's head was struck off, and the Bruce and his men galloped onwards.

It was now six years since the scuffle between Bruce and Comyn had taken place at Peebles. On February 10, 1306, they met again.

The Bruce arranged a meeting at the church of the Greyfriars at Dumfries, and there accused the Red Comyn of his treachery and broken faith.

"You lie!" said Comyn, and blows followed hot words.

We do not know who struck the first blow—it may have been Comyn—but daggers were drawn, and the Red Comyn fell, stabbed, before the altar.

As Bruce hurried out, his face showing the horror of what he had done, he met two of his friends, Lindsay and Kirkpatrick.

They eagerly asked how it was with him.

"Ill," said the Bruce, "for I doubt I have slain the Comyn."

"You doubt!" cried Kirkpatrick, "then I'll mak siccar!"

Rushing into the church, Kirkpatrick and Lindsay plunged their daggers into the wounded man's body, and also slew his uncle, Sir Robert Comyn, who tried to save him.

The church of the Greyfriars was desecrated. There was blood on the altar steps, the blood of a murdered man.

Robert Bruce had now not merely the English king for an enemy, and for enemies all the powerful friends of the man he had slain. The Pope of Rome and all the priests of the Romish Church were against a man who had committed what was to them so horrible and unpardonable a sin.

There was no going back for him now. No longer could he doubt and dally. Not only had he to fight for a crown and a country—he had to fight for his own life.

King Robert of Scotland

All over England and Scotland, like fire on a heather moor, went the news of the slaying of Comyn.

When King Edward heard it, his rage was very great. The Bruce had escaped him. He had slain the man who had betrayed him to the king. More than that, he and his followers had gone from the church of the Greyfriars to the castle of Dumfries, had turned out the English garrison, and had put a Scottish one in its place.

From Lochmaben Castle the Bruce called on the men of the Scottish borders, and on his friends in every part of the land, to come and help him to fight for a country and a crown.

And there was one man who joined him then, who, of all the friends Bruce ever knew, was the truest and the best.

Sir James Douglas was the son of Sir William Douglas, who was Governor of Berwick when it was sacked by the English. For years Sir William was a prisoner in chains, his lands were all taken from him, and in 1298 he died in the Tower of London.

Sir James was a tiny boy when the siege of Berwick took place, and his uncle, Lord Keith, was a father to him while his own father lay imprisoned in the Tower. The boy got his schooling at Glasgow, and in France, and was "the most complete and best accomplished young man in all Scotland or in any other land." We know him now as "the Good Lord James," but while he lived he was known and feared as "the Black Douglas." His dark hair and eyes won for him his name. He was tall and slim and pale. In company he was always sweet and gentle, talking with a little lisp. "When he was blythe, he was lufly" (they did not spell it "lovely" then), one old chronicler tells us, and he also tells us that, although he was so gentle and courteous and true that all men loved him, yet in battle his fearlessness made him a terrible enemy. From France he came to Scotland to be page to his kinsman, Bishop Lamberton of St. Andrews.

The bishop took him to see King Edward, and asked the king to restore to Douglas his father's lands and to give him a place at Court.

"I have given the lands to better men than you," said Edward roughly, "and had they not been given, still you should not have had them. I have no service for the sons of traitors." With a bitter heart Sir James went back to St. Andrews.

As soon as he heard that Bruce had slain Comyn, he rode off in haste to join him. In a lonely pass of Upper Tweeddale the Bruce, riding from Lochmaben to Glasgow, met and welcomed to his service the young knight, who never to his life's end bowed the knee to any king save

Robert, King of Scots. With not more than forty followers they rode on to Glasgow, where the Bishop of Glasgow joyfully welcomed Bruce as the man who was to fight for Scotland's freedom and to be Scotland's king.

From Glasgow Bruce went to Scone, the place where all the kings of Scotland were crowned.

The Stone of Destiny was in England, and there were no royal robes and no crown for the new king.

A golden coronella was hastily made, and the Bishop of Glasgow provided robes and a banner of the arras of the Scottish kings that he had had long concealed in his treasury.

It had always been the right of the earls of Fife to place the crown on a new king's head, but the earl of Fife served the King of England. Down from her castle in the north, a great retinue with her, came the Earl of Fife's sister, the Countess of Buchan. Her husband was a Comyn, but she cared for nothing but to do honour to the man who was to make Scotland a free country.

Robert the Bruce, then thirty-one years old, was crowned King of Scotland on March 27, 1306. Three bishops, one abbot, and three earls were the only great people of the land who were there to say "God save the King!"

But by his side he had his four sturdy brothers, the Black Douglas, his nephew Randolph, and a handful of other brave knights who were ready to draw their swords for their king and their country.

"Henceforth," said King Robert to his wife, "thou art Queen of Scotland, and I king."

"Alas!" she answered, "we are but King and Queen of the May! such as boys crown with flowers and rushes at the summer sports."

A king with a title and nothing else was the Bruce when the coronation was over.

King Edward, in the same fury of rage that made him massacre the people of Berwick, punished the Bruce every way that lay in his power. He gave his lands to others. His earldom of Carrick he took from him, and the earls who stood by Bruce as he was crowned also had their earldoms taken away. The earldom of Lennox was given to the traitor who had sold William Wallace.

The Earl of Buchan wished to kill his wife for crowning the Bruce, but Edward had for her a harder punishment. She was imprisoned, like a dangerous animal, in a huche, or iron cage, in a turret of Berwick Castle. Some chroniclers say that this cage dangled outside the walls for all the world to see. It seems more likely that the unhappy Countess was kept inside the walls, where no salt breezes from the North Sea could reach her, nor the song of the birds in the spring. There she died before the king she had crowned could set her free.

Edward was hunting in the New Forest when news of the Comyn's death reached him. From that day until he died, the Hammer of the Scots—as he called himself—hunted bigger game. He vowed he would conquer and humble the Scottish rebels, and punish without mercy "King Hobbe," as he scornfully nicknamed their king.

Such a conquest must have seemed an easy matter to Edward of England.

England was then, perhaps, the greatest power in Europe. Its navy ruled the seas. Its barons were united, and their followers were ready to fight and to die for them. The yeomanry helped to form a magnificent army—an army so strong, so brave, and so perfectly disciplined that not many years later it humbled France. Moreover, England was a very wealthy and prosperous country. The king knew that his treasuries could easily supply money enough to carry on a long war.

All these things were also known to Robert the Bruce. There was no army, no royal treasury behind King Robert. Yet, with only forty men at his back, he dared all.

In England Edward was scheming for Bruce's speedy overthrow. Orders were sent post haste to his generals in Scotland to have everything in train for war. More troops and more supplies were sent north. Edward was a great general as well as a great king, and it was not long ere his armies were ready to destroy Bruce and his little following.

At Whitsuntide a great feast was held at Westminster, when the Prince of Wales was knighted, along with 300 young noblemen.

It was then that King Edward swore a mighty oath. "By God and the swans" (emblems of faith and purity) he vowed that all the rest of his life should be spent in avenging the murder of Comyn, in hunting the Bruce and his followers to their death, and in breaking the spirit of rebellious Scotland.

At St. Paul's Cathedral a ceremony also took place for the humbling of Bruce. In a solemn service, where candles were lighted by the priests and then put out, Robert Bruce and three other knights were condemned for evermore as being the most wicked of sinners.

When the boggy lands of Scotland were golden with marsh buttercups, and when birds were singing in bracken and birch, an English army met with Bruce and his men in the woods of Methven in Perthshire.

The English outnumbered the Scots by 1500, and Bruce was taken by surprise.

A fierce fight took place, and Bruce led his men with splendid courage. Three times was a horse slain under him, and once he was taken prisoner, but the man who captured him was a Scottish knight who generously let him go. The grass grew red with the blood of brave men, and of all who fought there none fought more bravely than the Scottish king—

> "So hard and heavy dints he gave
> That where he came they made him way."

But vainly he fought, vainly rallied his men. The English were so strong that the Scots had to flee before them. Many brave knights were taken prisoners, and to them Edward showed no mercy. Some were hanged, some beheaded, one—the bravest of all—met with an even more cruel death, and his head was placed beside that of Wallace on London Bridge.

After this defeat, the common people did not dare to own the Bruce as their king. His only followers were a few trusty friends. With them, hiding in woods and on lonely mountain sides, he wandered northwards. Their clothes and shoes were sadly rent and worn by the time they reached Aberdeen.

"We are but King and Queen of the May," his wife had said at Scone.

What she had said now seemed to be true. All women whose husbands had fought for the Bruce were to be punished, commanded King Edward, and so the queen and her little daughter Marjory, Bruce's two sisters, and many other women joined Bruce at Aberdeen. An English army followed them there, and then they "took to the heather" with Bruce and his men.

Bruce's youngest brother, Nigel, though he was but a boy, took the ladies specially under his care. But the one who served them best of all was the Black Douglas. While they hid in woods and on moors and hills where the English with their heavy horses could not follow them, it was Douglas who was best at tracking and slaying the red deer for their food. His skillful hands made nets and rods and caught salmon, trout, eels, and even—when they were hard pressed—minnows. And ever he was so gay, so brave, and so sure that in the end all must go well, that he always brought comfort and hope to the Bruce's heart.

Bruce the Outlaw

From the woods of the Dee and the Don, Bruce and his little band wandered to the wilds of the west country.

The fish and game that they caught were their chief food, for the people feared the English king too much to feed his enemies. Often they were hungry; always they were in danger.

At length they came to the country of Lorn, but John MacDougall, Lord of Lorn, was uncle of the Red Comyn, and with 1000 men came out to slay the Bruce and those with him.

At a place still called Dalry—the King's Field—there was a fierce fight. Bruce lost several of his men, and the Black Douglas was wounded. Fearing that his little army would be cut in pieces, Bruce made them retreat through a narrow pass, "between a loch side and a brae." He himself came last of all, and all those of the enemy who tried to force their way through the pass in pursuit fell before his sword.

Three brothers named Macindrosser, or "sons of the doorkeeper," swore they would slay the Bruce.

One of them snatched at his bridle rein, but Bruce shore his arm off by the shoulder and he bled to death.

The second gripped him by the leg. Rising in his stirrups, Bruce drove his spurs into his horse's sides, and the horse, rearing upwards, dashed down the man with its hoofs. As he tried to rise, down swept the Bruce's sword and cleft his head in two. The third leaped up behind Bruce on his horse, and grasped him so tightly by his mantle that the king could not swing his long sword. But from behind him, with a grasp of iron, and muscles all a-strain, Bruce dragged the man, and with one great blow of his battle-axe dashed out his brains.

The dead man's hand still clung to the Bruce's mantle with so firm a clasp that Bruce had to undo the great brooch that fastened it, and leave it to be a possession of the MacDougalls of Lorn even to this day.

After the defeat of Dalry, Bruce's followers grew very down-hearted. But always he would cheer them and keep them from despair.

"Think how many men have been in far harder straits than we," he said, "and yet God helped them through. Let us bravely withstand our foes, and prefer death to a coward's life."

Then he would tell them stories of the heroes of old, and of all the hard things they had to do and to endure before victory was theirs.

But although men were able to hold out through their wanderings in lonely places, often without food, always without a right house to sleep in, it was more than women could do. Winter was coming on; the autumn nights were long and chill; the woods no longer gave much shelter, and the bitter sleet showers drenched them through. Their strength gave in, and Bruce was forced to say good-bye to his wife and little daughter, and send them and the other ladies to his castle of Kildrummie in Aberdeenshire. His youngest brother, Nigel, went with them, and the parting was a sad one between Bruce and those that he loved so dearly. As he watched his wife ride off on his own horse that he had given to her, he little thought that it would be nine long years before they met again.

From England, meantime, a great army, led by the Prince of Wales and many of his new-made knights, marched northward.

They were a gallant company. Their armour was magnificent. Their clothing was of the finest silk. The prince's pennons were of beaten gold. Lest the wild Scots should give him too little sport, he took his falcons with him, and amused himself by hawking, netting partridges, playing dice, and jesting with his court fool. A lion was a part of his escort.

Nigel Bruce, with the ladies under his care, safely reached Kildrummie. It was a strong castle, and they had plenty of provisions, so that when the prince and his great army came to besiege it, Nigel was not afraid.

Again and again the besiegers were driven back. But one of the garrison of the castle was a base traitor. Into their store of grain he threw a red-hot ploughshare, and with a rush and a roar, and with blinding clouds of smoke, the flames blazed up. The garrison ran to the battlements to escape being burned alive, but the fire was too fierce for the English to take the castle, and the Scots defended it gallantly. But now they had two foes to fight. Outside were the English; inside was starvation. The greedy flames had devoured their stores. At day-break next morning the Scots were forced to surrender.

Before the siege the queen, Princess Marjory, the Bruce's sisters, and some others had sought refuge in a monastery at Tain. They were now given up to the English, and taken to England to drag out the weary days in "cages," like those in which the Countess of Buchan was imprisoned.

Sir Nigel Bruce, a handsome, gallant boy, was taken, with several other knights, to Berwick. There he was hanged, drawn, and beheaded.

Later on, two of the Bruce's other brothers, Thomas and Alexander, while on their way to Carrick, were taken prisoners, and put to death at Carlisle in the same cruel way as their young brother.

When the Bruce had parted from his wife and little girl, he and his followers, on foot, and not 200 in all, kept to the hills in the west. From hunger and cold and wet they suffered sadly, and at length it was decided to make for the Mull of Kintyre, away to the south.

Sir Niall Campbell, whose country it was, was sent on before them to get boats and food, and to meet them at the Firth of Clyde.

Meantime Bruce and the rest of his company came by Loch Lomond, where good hiding was to be had in the thick woods of fir and hazel and birch, where the bracken grows feet high. But on the shores of the loch no boat was to be found. Round and round the loch side they searched in vain, until at last Douglas came on a little water-logged boat sunk near the shore. Speedily it was brought to land and baled out, but it was so small that only three men could go in it at a time. Some of the hardy men of the hills swam across, their arms and clothes tied in bundles on their heads, and in a day and a night the others were ferried over. It was winter weather, the men were tired and hungry, and the boat could not have been oversafe. But the king made light of all discomforts, and cheered up those with whom he crossed by reading to them an old romance of a brave knight called Ferambras, and of the trials he endured.

Next day the Earl of Lennox, whose lands lay at the other side of the loch, heard that poachers were out after the deer in his woods, and went off to catch them. Soon he heard the sound of a horn, and at once he knew that it was the King of Scotland who gave that ringing call. He hastened through the woods to where the Bruce had slain a deer, and when they met he wept for joy, while Bruce—

> "For pity wept again
> That never of meeting was so fain."

When the Bruce and his hungry followers had had more and better food spread before them than they had seen for many a day, they, and Lennox with them, went on to the shores of Clyde. They found Niall Campbell awaiting them with a little fleet of boats, well stocked with food.

Great strong fists that had been well used to hold spears now held oars. Well and steadily the men rowed across the cold grey water, past the isle of Arran, to Kintyre in the western sea.

The Earl of Lennox, with his little galley, let the others be well on their way before he started.

He had not long left the land when, behind him, he saw the galleys of the Bruce's enemy, John of Lorn, coming in hot pursuit. Quickly they gained on him, and Lennox threw one piece of his luggage overboard after another to lighten his boat. The greedy men of Lorn could not bear to see such plunder drift past without stopping to pick it up.

Each time they stopped meant a gain for Lennox, and speedily the lightened boat cut through the water until the galleys of the enemy were only specks, far away.

Angus, Lord of Kintyre, gave Bruce and his followers a kind welcome, and for three days they stayed with him at his castle of Dunaverty, on a steep cliff above the sea.

It was lucky for Bruce that on the third day he left Kintyre for Rachrin (now Rathlin), a bleak and wind-swept little island on the Irish coast.

For, while his boats were still fighting their way west-ward, through rough seas and stormy weather, Lorn's galleys had come to Kintyre, and very soon an English army was besieging Dunaverty.

At Rachrin news came to the Bruce of the taking of Kildrummie, the imprisonment of his wife and little daughter, and the execution of his brave young brother.

It was a dreary winter for the hunted king. All Scotland swarmed with his enemies. His brothers and some of his truest friends had been slain. His wife, child, and sisters were in captivity. He and his handful of true men had to shelter in the poorest of huts, amongst the wild Irish people, who were then almost savages, and from whom they could only get food of the roughest.

It was at this time, when despair must have been very near him, that a story that you must know well is told of Robert the Bruce.

One day he sat in the wretched little cabin of turf that was then his home, wondering if it would not be best, after all, to give up his fight for Scotland that seemed to pass from one failure to another, and to go with the Douglas and his other friends to fight against the Saracens. He might then, he thought, win forgiveness from his Church for the murder of Comyn. Just then he noticed a spider dangling down on its silvery thread. This spider was trying to swing itself across from one cobwebbed rafter to another, but each time it tried, it failed. Six times did Bruce count its attempts.

"Six times," thought he, "and six times have I also been defeated. If the little spider has the patience to try again, then why should not I?"

Eagerly he watched it dangling, and once again it tried.

The seventh attempt swung it to the place where it wished to be, and it went happily on with its work, little knowing that it had settled the fate of a kingdom.

A seventh time Bruce also tried, and victory from that time was his.

And that is why people who live north of the Tweed will always try to prevent you from killing a spider.

Meantime the Black Douglas grew weary of a winter spent in doing nothing on an Irish island, while there was plenty of fighting to be had in his own Scottish land.

"Let us cross to Arran," he said to another knight, Sir Robert Boyd. "Instead of idly living on food brought us by the poor people of Rachrin, we will go to Brodick Castle and see what our swords will gain for us there."

They got leave from the king, crossed to Kintyre, and at nightfall rowed past the land and on to Arran.

Day had not dawned when they reached the island and drew their boat ashore. Under one of those banks where hazels and silver birches and heather and bog myrtle come so near the shore that on stormy days they are lashed with the salt sea spray, they hid the boat. They were wet and weary and hungry, but through the night they tramped on, till they came to Brodick Castle, under the shadow of Goat Fell.

The English knight who kept the castle had with him many guests. On the evening of the night before three boats, laden with stores, clothing, wines, and food for the castle, arrived in Brodick Bay. From their hiding-place

Douglas and his men watched the sailors and some of the garrison unlading these boats and toiling up to the castle laden with stores. Then, from the trees, there burst a little band of fierce fighting men.

"A Douglas! a Douglas!" they cried, and those who did not fall before their swords fled in confusion, leaving behind them so handsome a store of arms, food, wines, and clothing, that the Scots had enough to enable them to hold out for many a week against the English garrison.

News of the Douglas's successful raid was sent to Rachrin, and ten days later the Bruce and the rest of his men arrived in thirty-three small galleys.

He asked a woman of the island if she had seen any armed strangers, and she led him to a wooded glen.

"Here I saw the men you ask after," said she. Bruce blew on his horn three blasts that echoed up the glen.

"That is the king!" cried Douglas, "I know his blast of old!"

Joyfully they hastened to greet the Bruce.

> "And blithely welcomed them the king,
> That joyful was of their meeting."

In Arran, with its hills and moors, and deep wooded glens and corries, Bruce might for long have withstood his enemies.

But five-and-twenty miles across the sea, to the south-east, lay the Bruce's own land of Carrick. On clear days, from the Arran hills, he could trace each outline of the coast, and even see the blue smoke rising up from the chimneys at Turnberry, the castle that, in spite of the King of England, he called his own.

When birds were singing in the bushes, and the blackthorns were in bloom, the Bruce sent to Carrick a spy, one Cuthbert.

"If the people of Carrick are my friends," said the Bruce, "then on the day I now fix make a fire on Turnberry Nook, that we may know that it is safe for us to cross over."

But when Cuthbert got to his king's own land he found that no man dared own Robert the Bruce as his lord.

Turnberry Castle was held by an English knight, Sir Henry Percy, with 300 men, and the poor people so feared him that they dared do nothing to displease him.

"I can light no fire," thought Cuthbert, and sadly waited for a chance of returning to Arran. But chance did for the Bruce what Cuthbert left undone.

How it happened, no one knows, but on the night that Bruce and his men eagerly looked across the sea to Turnberry for a red blaze rushing skywards, there was a mistake made such as was made in Scotland 500 years later, when the "False Alarm" showed all Europe the stuff of which Scotsmen are made.

The Bruce's heart must have beat fast when he saw the red glare. No time was lost in starting their boats, and all night they rowed. It was still dark when they landed, and were met by Cuthbert with woe on his face.

"There are only enemies here, Sir King," he said. "The fire was never kindled by me."

Then the king held a council with his knights.

"What is best for us to do?" he asked.

Up spoke his brother Edward, as strong a man as the Bruce himself, and one who was ever more rash.

"I have had enough of the sea!" said Edward Bruce. "Come good, come ill, I take my adventure here."

To this the Bruce agreed.

In the hamlet round the castle, all was dark and silent. In the darkness the Scots were able to slip noiselessly upon the sleeping English, who only knew that death was upon them when fierce hands were on their throats and swords at their hearts.

In the castle Sir Henry Percy heard the cries of dying men and the din of fighting. But he and his garrison dared not come out to face what seemed to them, in the blackness of night, an enormous conquering army.

With Percy's horses, and much other rich spoil of silver, arms, and clothing, Bruce and his men hastened deeper into the wilds of Carrick, to find fastnesses in the wooded hills.

How Robert the Bruce Met his Enemies

While the Bruce was hiding in Carrick, King Edward and his generals were spreading their forces all over Scotland. In February and March 1307, 4000 English foot soldiers had mustered at Carlisle. If you look at the map at the beginning of this volume, you will see that it seemed as likely that King Robert would escape from his enemies as that a fly will safely wing its way out from amongst the thousand cobwebs that clog the rafters of a barn.

Nor was it only from his openly avowed enemies that Bruce was in danger. Again and again there were traitors in his camp.

In Carrick dwelt a one-eyed man who made Bruce believe that he and his two sons were his friends.

An English general sent for him, and got him to agree to sell the king for £40 worth of land. This ruffian knew that it was the custom of the Bruce to go out for an early morning walk, armed only with his sword, and with none but a little page for company. So one morning he and his sons lay in wait in a thicket. As the king came in sight they sprang out, the father with a sword, one son with a sword and axe, the other with a spear.

"These men come to slay us!" said the king to his page. "What weapon hast thou?"

"Ah, sire," said the boy, "I have only a bow and arrows."

"Quickly give them to me," said the Bruce, and stand aside."

"Traitor!" called he to the one-eyed man, "thou hast sold me. Come no nearer!"

"Who should come near to thee but I?" said the man, still pretending to be the Bruce's friend, and always drawing nearer to where he stood.

"Come at the risk of your life!" shouted the Bruce.

And when the man and his sons still came on, he bent the page's bow, and aimed so well that the arrow smote the man's one eye, pierced his brain, and he fell dead. The two sons then rushed on the king. He with the battle-axe fetched a fierce blow at him, but, before it could fall, the Bruce with his sword cleft his head in two. The other man lunged at him with his spear, but, as the spear was about to strike, the Bruce with his sword cut off its steel point as one cuts thistle-heads off with a walking-stick. Then, with another mighty blow, the king laid the third of the traitors dead and bleeding at his feet.

He was wiping the blood from his trusty sword when the little page ran up, overjoyed to find the three men dead.

"These had been three gallant men," said the Bruce, "had they been loyal ones."

It was little wonder that his own followers loved the Bruce as few great kings have ever been loved.

He was what we call "every inch a king." He was taller than most men, handsomer, and stronger. He had yellow hair, and blue and sparkling eyes, and instead of speaking to the Scots in the Anglo-French, or the French used by knights of his day, he would always speak to them in the Scots tongue that they themselves used. To women he was ever courteous and gentle, and he was always thoughtful for those who were less strong than he. The hunted outlaw, who had to shelter in the thick fir woods, or on the heather moors of Carrick and Galloway, where the brown mountain burns tumble over the stones in deep cuttings between the hills, and where bracken hid the doorway of the cave that sheltered him, was a man who knew no fear. When those beside him lost heart he was ever ready to cheer them. No defeat could break his spirit, nor prevent him from seeing the amusing side of things. No hardship could conquer his dauntless bravery.

While Edward's forces hemmed him in on every side, it was not safe to keep more than a handful of men beside him, nor was it possible to provide food for more than a few. Often he was all alone.

This was the time for John of Lorn, who had defeated him at Dalry, to defeat him in real earnest.

Lorn had brought with him to Galloway a famous

bloodhound, that had once belonged to Bruce, and which was very fond of him.

"Now I have him!" thought Lorn.

Almost at once the dog got on the trail of his old master, and joyfully threw up his head to give the deep-toned bay that is so terrible a sound to those who are chased by bloodhounds.

Bruce made his party scatter and seek safety, and kept with him only two men. To a bog beside a stream, near where his troop of sixty had crossed in making their escape, Bruce went and waited. It was night, and the sound of running water, the baying of the dog, and the cry of a startled curlew, were at first the only sounds to be heard.

"Go, lie down and rest," said he to his two companions. "I myself will watch here."

"But, sire," said they, "who will watch with you?"

"God," he said. "Pass on. I will have it so."

All alone, then, he watched by the stream, while nearer and nearer came the baying of the hound.

The moon rose as he watched, and from afar he could hear the clatter of horses' hoofs, the clang of harness and armour, and the murmur of voices.

Bruce then woke his two men. With them he crossed the stream, and sent them on to alarm the others, and make them flee onwards.

Alone he stood by the ford, and saw the moon gleam on two hundred spears. Two hundred men to one was heavy odds, but the one man was Robert the Bruce. The ford was narrow, and the men had to come one at a time. But they saw only a solitary sentinel on the river's bank, and plunged fearlessly into the water. The first horse was scrambling up the broken bank, when a drive from the Bruce's spear made its rider fall back dead into the stream. The horse was stabbed by a swift second thrust, and, rolling backwards, blocked up the way for the horseman who followed. One by one horses and men splashed through the ford, and tried to gain the bank. One by one they fell back dead, or wounded so sorely that they had no strength left to fight for their lives, but drifted down in the current, and were drowned in the swift-flowing river. Fourteen men were slain by his spear by the time his followers came to the rescue and drove back their enemies in confusion.

But John of Lorn was not one to give in. He waited a little, and again, when his own force was of 800 and the Bruce's numbered only 300, he set the bloodhound on the track of his master.

Bruce broke up his little army into three companies and made them leave him and retreat by different ways. With him he kept one man only, his foster-brother.

Lorn, knowing from the baying of the dog and the way in which it strained at its leash that the Bruce was near, picked out five Highlanders, fleet of foot, and bade them run him down.

Standing like stags at bay, they found the two hunted

men. Three of them attacked the king; the two others fell on his foster-brother.

It was a fierce fight and a short one. Four men were slain by the Bruce's sword. His foster-brother slew the fifth.

"Thou hast helped right gallantly!" said the Bruce.

"It is like you to say so!" said the foster-brother, "when you slew four, and I only one!"

But the danger was not yet over. John of Lorn and his other men were near, and the dog was baying savagely.

Onward hurried Bruce and his friend—ever onward, through thick wood, bog, and brushwood.

"I can go no further," at last said the king, his strength all gone.

But his brave foster-brother would not allow him to give in, and on, once more, they stumbled. A little river ran through the wood they were in. Into this they dropped and waded down it. They heard the dog come to where they had entered the stream, but soon came dismal howls, showing that the running water had baffled it. It had lost the trail, and John of Lorn and his men had to go homeward, cursing the more when they found the dead bodies of the five Highlanders.

After a short rest Bruce and his foster-brother went on. They were saved for this once, they knew, but the hunt was up; they must speedily find a shelter.

Leaving the wood, they crossed a wide moor, and there

met with three ill-looking men, armed with swords and axes, and one of them carrying a sheep on his back.

"Whither do you go?" asked the king.

"We seek Robert the Bruce," they answered, "for we would join with him."

"If that be your will," said the Bruce, " come with me, and I will show him to you."

At once the face of the man who had spoken changed, and Bruce was sure that they were his enemies and meant him no good.

"Until we are better acquainted," said he, " you must go before us, and we will follow near you."

"You have no reason to think we mean you any ill," grumbled the man.

"Go on," said the king, "it is my will to travel so." And they obeyed the Bruce, as he made most men do.

As night was falling, they came to the ruins of a hut. There a sheep was killed, and a fire to roast it kindled.

The king and his foster-brother lit a fire for themselves at the other end of the hut from the strangers, the men sulkily watching them as they did so.

It was long since the king had tasted food, and they all ate hungrily of the broiled mutton. The food and the warmth of the fire, after the long day and night they had had of hard travel, fighting, and anxiety, made Bruce so heavy with sleep that he could scarcely keep his eyes open. He arranged with his foster-brother that they should watch time about, the latter taking the first watch. But the brave man was so tired that scarcely had the king's eyes closed, than he slept too.

No sooner did the traitors see them asleep, than they crept towards them, to murder them ere they could awake. But the king slept lightly, and the slight noise they made as they came near him awoke him. He sprang to his feet, and in the red fire-light saw the three murderers almost upon him. With a kick he awoke his foster-brother, but before Bruce's faithful friend could more than half rise from the ground, he was stabbed, and fell back dead. Three to one it was now; three men fresh and untired, against one who was weary and worn out. But, one after another, the murderers fell before his sword.

There were three dead men, who well deserved to be slain, lying beside Bruce's friend in that lonely cottage on the moor when Bruce came away from it.

On through the hills, to the place where he had told his men to meet him, the Bruce, with aching limbs and a heavy heart for the loss of a man he loved, then took his way.

Near lonely Loch Dee there is still to be seen a hill called Craigencallie, or "the Old Woman's Crag." Here it was that the meeting had been fixed.

An old woman lived in a cottage on the hill. She had been three times married, and by each husband had a son. Their names were Murdoch, MacKie, and MacLurg. It was not yet dawn when the Bruce arrived, but the woman met him fearlessly.

"Who are you?" she asked. "From whence do you come? and whither do you go?"

"I am a traveller," he said, "journeying through the country."

"All travellers," said the old woman, "are welcome here for the sake of one."

"And who may he be, good dame?" asked the king.

"I'll tell thee that," said the woman. "Good King Robert the Bruce is he, the rightful lord of this country. His foes press him hard, but before very long I hope to see him lord and king over all the land."

"Do you then love him so well?" asked the Bruce.

"In truth I do," she answered

"You see him before you," said the king. "I am Robert the Bruce."

A proud woman was the old woman of Craigencallie that day. While the king ate and drank of her best, her sons came in and were presented to their king.

"You shall take my sons for your men, sire," said she.

The king asked if his new liegemen were good bowmen. To show him what they could do, they fetched their bows, and first of all Murdoch let fly at two ravens sitting on a crag, and drove the one arrow through them both. MacKie shot next, and killed a raven flying overhead, but MacLurg missed his mark.

In happier days, the Bruce, then "lord and king over all the land," asked the old woman what he could do for her to show his gratitude for her goodness to him in his evil days.

"Just give me," said she, "the wee bit hassock o' land atween Palmure and Penkiln."

The "hassock" was about five miles long and three broad, and was divided amongst the three sons. And if you look at the coat-of-arms of the Murdochs of Cumloden and the Murdochs of Gartincaber, and the branches of their family, you will find a raven with an arrow driven through its breast.

While Bruce talked to Murdoch and the others, Douglas and Edward Bruce came to Craigencallie, and before long 150 of the king's men had mustered there.

When the Bruce had told them his adventures since they parted, he asked for news of the enemy.

"They must think us so scattered," said he, "that they are likely to keep careless watch, so that it will be easy to surprise them."

"That is true," said the Douglas. "On my way here I passed close to a company of 200 of them, bivouacked so carelessly on Raploch Moss that a surprise will be very easy."

At nightfall the king and his men were on the march to Raploch. It was grey dawn when they came to where the English lay, and before the sun was high in the sky the moss was strewn with dead men. Before they were well awake, the swords of Bruce and his men laid them low. Those who were able to fly, fled in wild confusion.

When Edward of England, growing old, and wasting away from illness, heard of Bruce these tales, and very many more, he must have ground his teeth with rage at the success and dauntless valour of his enemy, "King Hobbe."

Victories for Bruce, and the Death of King Edward

While the Bruce was having adventure after adventure in his own kingdom, King Edward lay idle and useless at Carlisle. Mortal illness kept him from crossing the Border to humble his enemy, as he believed he was sure to do.

In March 1307, when snow lay on the Galloway moors and uplands, an English general, De Valence, resolved that he would gain a victory that would gladden the sick king's heart.

Bruce was known to be in hiding in lonely Glen Trool, and De Valence bribed a woman to go up the glen and find out where Bruce and his men were sheltering. He, and a large, well-armed force, followed their spy. But the Bruce knew a spy when he saw one. The woman was threatened with death unless she confessed all. She told the king that De Valence was coming behind her up the glen.

From what is still called "the King's Seat," a ledge on a mountain above Glen Trool, the Bruce watched the English army coming to take him. On either side of the loch the mountains run down so sharply into the water that there is but a narrow path for men to pass by, one at a time.

The Bruce made his men hide in the woods on these mountains, and himself kept guard above. Onward and upward came the English, clambering slowly and with difficulty up the narrow foothold by the loch side. No sign was to be seen of Bruce and his men until an arrow from the king's bow made the first Englishman leap in the air with a choking cry and roll over like a shot rabbit. Then, from far up the mountain side, came the clear call of a bugle. It was the Bruce who sounded it, and at once, as though it had been a fairy horn, the woods became alive with armed men. Stones and arrows rained down on the English soldiers. Great boulders crashed through the trees and swept the English, maimed and senseless, into the waters of the lake. The path was too narrow for those behind to help those in front, and so the slaughter went on until what was left of 1500 men had to flee in terror before 300.

Even now you may see a green strip between the brown mountains and the dark waters of Loch Trool, and you will find that the country people call it "the Soldiers' Holm," for they say that it was there that De Valence's men were buried.

For Bruce the victory meant much. The Scottish people began to flock to his standard.

"It now appears," says one old writer, "that he has the right, and God is openly for him."

On May to, 1307, yet another victory was his. In Clydesdale the Black Douglas had laid an ambush for De Moubray, an English general, and had routed him and his men with great slaughter.

De Valence heard the tale of this defeat with much wrath, and proudly sent Bruce a challenge to come down from the hills with his men and fight his army in open field.

Bruce accepted the challenge. On Loudon Moor the two armies met.

Bruce had with him about 600 fighting men, and about the same number of "rangale" (rabble), while De Valence had 3000 well-armed, well-trained soldiers. Between two peat mosses, at "a yellow, benty, mossy, boggy place," Bruce posted his men, and there dug three deep trenches.

A flight of arrows from the English yeomen did little harm to men protected in trenches—of a rougher sort than those that our soldiers had in the Crimea—and De Valence led his horsemen, their armour gleaming in the sun, dashingly across the "haughs," down the course of a little hill burn, in a splendid cavalry charge. But the Scots grimly met the horsemen with a solid hedge of pikes. The horses, hideously wounded, swerved, screamed in pain and terror, and galloped back riderless, throwing the rest of De Valence's army into wild confusion.

It was then Bruce's turn to charge, and this he and his men did so successfully that before the day was done—

"The field was well nigh covered all. Both with slain horses and with men."

The English army, in shameful flight, was pursued by the Scots, who took many prisoners. The king was no longer captain of a band of outlaws, lurking in woods and in caves of the hills. He was general of an army that could meet 3000 Englishmen in the open field and win a gallant victory.

Three days later he defeated another English general, Sir Ralph de Monthermer, who had to seek refuge in Ayr Castle.

The news of these victories reached King Edward at Carlisle. He was furious with his generals because of their defeat. No longer would he leave the humbling of "King Hobbe" to them. He must rise from his sick bed and march to Scotland.

On the march, his last sickness came upon him. He was dying when, on July 6, he reached Burgh-on-Sands, a little town on the Solway from whence he could look across the grey water at the land he had tried in vain to conquer.

"What town is this?" he asked.

"They call it Burgh-on-Sands, sire," they answered.

"I thought to reach the burgh of Jerusalem," said he. "I thought of no other burgh."

Then, in pain and mortal weakness, he sent for his son Edward, Prince of Wales. In the presence of all the barons, Edward made the prince swear that he would take his heart to the Holy Land and there bury it, but that his bones should be carried at the head of the English army until Scotland was a conquered land.

On July 7 he died, but the new king, Edward II., paid no heed to his dead father's wishes, nor to the oath he had sworn.

In Westminster they laid the body of the man who was so brave, so ambitious, and so great a king, and so cruel an enemy.

On his tomb they carved words that he himself had chosen

EDVARDVS: PRIMVS:

SCOTTORVM: MALLEVS:

HIC: EST: PACTVM: SERVA.

"Here is the first Edward, Hammer of the Scots. Keep Covenant."

Of the new king, Bruce said that he feared the dead king's bones more than Edward II.'s living body.

The Scots hated Edward I., but they feared him. To those whom he judged by his laws to have been disloyal to him he was mercilessly cruel. They were burned to death, hanged, or torn to pieces at the heels of horses. But now the Hammer of the Scots was dead, and his son was a man that his enemies despised.

And now, too, those who hated England and the English had for their king a true and noble knight, without fear and without reproach. In those hard days when alone, cold, hungry, and tired out, body and soul, he had had to clamber barefoot—for often his shoes were worn out—to some mountain shelter, or had had for weeks at a time to live only on roots, and water from some spring in the hills, the Bruce had learned to forget himself, to endure without complaint, pain and bitter hardship. And he who has learned perfectly how to govern himself must ever be a very perfect leader of men.

In August Edward II. carried out his father's wishes so far, by leading an army into Ayrshire. But a few weeks of campaigning wearied him, and, without fighting, he went back to London, where he found things that amused him more.

No sooner had he gone than the men of Tweeddale, Teviotdale, and Ettrick Forest threw off all pretence of being loyal to Edward. They rose in force, and the English who lived on the Border fled in terror into England.

Early in the winter of 1307 Bruce marched northwards, leaving the Black Douglas behind him to guard the Border.

"I love better to hear the lark sing than the mouse cheep," said the Douglas; but when castles were to be taken, he was always ready.

While he fought and won on the Border, the Bruce lay at Inverurie in Aberdeenshire, a very sick and weary man.

His spirit was strong to withstand hunger, cold, stormy weather, constant anxiety, want of rest, peril, and suffering. His bravery and good-humour never failed. But the years of hardship had worn him out. His health broke down, and for weeks he lay at death's door.

His men began to lose heart. Without Bruce to lead them they dared not face an English army. When they heard that John Comyn, Earl of Buchan, and many English and Scottish nobles were coming against them, they marched across the hills to a place called Slioch, bearing the king on a litter.

The snow lay deep; they had brought little food with them, and after three days, during which the English and Scottish archers shot at each other, Edward Bruce, who held command while his brother lay sick, brought his little army back to Inverurie. Slowly, with the king's litter in the centre of a column, the march was made, in full view of the English army. They out-numbered the Scots by two to one, yet no attack was made.

Before daybreak, on Christmas Eve 1307, Buchan attacked the Bruce's outposts at Inverurie, slaying some of his men, and making the others fly before him.

When this news reached the king, he rose from his bed.

"No medicine could have cured me as this has done," said he.

Though still so weak that two men had to hold him up, he had his armour buckled on, and was helped on to his horse. Then, "with a cheerful countenance," he "hastened with his army against the enemy, to the battle-ground."

The mere sight of the Bruce, whom they believed to be dying, leading an army, was too much for Buchan's men, who were triumphantly routed. The fight seemed to cure the king, for from that day he got well.

In May of that year, at Old Meldrum, he surprised and defeated Buchan, burning and laying waste his lands. In no way did he spare his old enemy. It is said that thirty of the Comyns were beheaded in one day. Their grave is still known as "The Grave of the Headless Comyns."

To this day charred trunks of trees are found in the northern mosses to remind us of the "Herschip (or Harrying) of Buchan."

How Edward II and Robert the Bruce Did their Campaigning

Leaving blackened moors and woods and smoking ruins behind him, Bruce marched southwards.

In those days Scotland was thickly studded with castles—most of them sturdy little grey peel towers, perched upon rocks—and within a year of Edward I.'s death, Bruce had destroyed 137 of them.

It was then only the Scottish cathedrals and a few castles belonging to very great lords that were large and beautiful. The towns consisted mostly of wooden buildings. Many of the churches were made of oak and thatched with straw. Even the bridges were wooden, and the hovels of the peasantry were built of turf and twigs, so that it was easy for a conqueror to burn down the towns and villages that fell before him.

Bruce's army always travelled light. No heavy baggage waggons with rich stock of wines and provisions lumbered after them, keeping them from hastening onwards. Each man had behind his saddle a little sack of oatmeal, a "girdle," or flat iron plate upon which to bake himself oat-cakes, and some strips of dried flesh, like the biltong of the Boers. If their stock of meat gave out, they killed some of the black cattle, or sheep, or pigs they came upon, or the red deer of the hills, or, it might be, the oxen that then drew ploughs and waggons, and roasted them in their skins. For drink they had the pure water of the burns and rivers. The English kings with their great retinue were as sorely handicapped by these light horse-men as the Britons were by the Boers a few years ago, when the war in South Africa first began. The English took with them all the means for turning a campaign in an enemy's country into a prolonged picnic. In 1300 Edward I. brought his own nets and fishermen to Scotland to supply his royal table.

Aberdeen fell before the Bruce, and Forfar Castle. Perth was less easily taken.

In chill winter weather Bruce laid siege to it, but its walls were strong, and it was well defended.

For six weeks "bickerings" went on between the besieged and besiegers. Then, amidst the jeers of the garrison, Bruce marched his men away. His general's eye had seen that open assault would never take the town, and he had noted well the point where the defence was weakest.

On the eighth night after they left, under cover of darkness, Bruce and his men came back again.

Carrying scaling-ladders, they made for the part of the moat that Bruce's quick eye had noticed.

With his lance shaft Bruce sounded the moat until he

found a place where the water was only throat-high. It was an icy bath for a January night, and a dangerous one, but in he plunged, carrying a ladder with him. A French knight in his company crossed himself for wonder at the sight. "What shall we say of our lords of France!" he exclaimed, "when a king of such chivalry as this—

> "'In such peril has him set
> To win a wretched hamlet!'"

With that he leapt into the moat after the king. The king's men quickly followed. They plunged into the water up to their necks, put up their ladders, and scaled the walls. The sentinels were taken unawares. The Scots, pouring into the town, soon had the sleeping, or sleepy, garrison at their mercy. They slew only a few men, but they tumbled down walls and towers, took much rich booty of arms and merchandise, and marched away to further victories.

Early in the same year the Bruce's castle of Lochmaben became his own once more, and the other castles of Annandale soon fell before him.

The Black Douglas was also winning victories. One night he came to a house on Lyne Water in Tweeddale, meaning to shelter there until morning with his men. He found other armed men there before him. As he stood by the window he could clearly hear what they said, and knew one voice to be that of Thomas Randolph, the Bruce's nephew.

Randolph had fought for his uncle when Bruce's warfare first began, but was taken prisoner at Methven. To save his head he then joined the English, and since then had helped John of Lorn and many another to hunt and harry the Bruce.

The Douglas signed to his men to surround the house. Ere those inside could grip their swords, the door was burst open, and the slogan of "A Douglas! a Douglas!" told them into whose hands they had fallen. There was a fierce fight. In the darkness some men escaped, but Randolph was one of the prisoners taken.

When Randolph was brought before the king, "You have been unfaithful to me for some time," said the Bruce, "but now you must be my friend again."

Randolph was as hot-tempered as he was brave, and he rudely answered his uncle.

"You challenged the King of England to open warfare!" he said, "and yet you stoop to unknightly tricks."

"Since you speak so rudely and with such proud words," said the Bruce quietly, "it will be well for you to go to prison until you have learned how to behave."

So to prison Randolph went for a time. But it was not long before the Black Douglas had a rival in brave and daring deeds, gladly and fearlessly done for the king by his trusty knight, Sir Thomas Randolph.

In Galloway Edward Bruce was winning fights. One by one the English garrisons were driven out, until thirteen castles had been taken by Edward Bruce. Before the end of the year 1308 the Border land was almost all won to King Robert.

In 1309, when March winds were blowing shrewdly down the passes in the western hills, the Bruce came to grips with his old enemy, John of Lorn.

Lorn now stationed his force of 2000 men on a steep hillside, just above the narrow gorge where the waters of Loch Awe rush down the Pass of Brander. He himself stayed in his boat on Loch Etive. Round a spur of Ben Cruachan, in the rear of the men of Lorn, Bruce sent Douglas and a company of archers. With the rest of his men he entered the Pass. They were met by a hail of arrows from the enemy, and by a murderous storm of great stones, sent crashing down the hillside upon them. But quickly the Bruce's little army charged up the hill—as Scottish regiments since have charged at Alma and Dargai—and soon were fighting hand to hand with the men of Lorn. Then, from the mountain above them, came the ringing cry, "A Douglas! a Douglas!" and Douglas and his archers bore down on the enemy from the rear. Many a clansman lay on the hillside that day, sleeping never to wake. Those who could rushed to a bridge over the Awe, but the bridge was won by Bruce's men. The men of Lorn were slain or drowned. John of Lorn had to make for the sea in his galley, while his country was wasted by the king he had tried to hunt to his death.

Later on in the year, Bruce took Dunstaffnage Castle at Oban, the stronghold of Lorn's clan, and John of Lorn had to fly to England, and never had a home in Scotland again.

While Bruce and his men were driving their foes before them, Edward of England was feebly deciding on ways of treating Scotland, and as feebly changing his mind. Robert the Bruce had friends. Edward had favourites, and his selfish love of pleasure made him do just as these men—especially one man named Piers Gaveston—wished.

In September 1310 he at length resolved to invade Scotland, and marched across the Border, by way of St. Boswells and Selkirk, as far as Linlithgow.

It was a bad year for campaigning. In Scotland famine had wrecked the land, and horse-flesh was being used for food.

In front of the invading army, with its cumbrous following of all the luxurious things that Edward wanted, went Bruce and his force of light horse and hardy infantry. They "lifted" all the cattle they came to, like the Border raiders of later days, and drove them before them, so that no fresh beef was to be found to supply King Edward and his forces.

From every side they seemed ready to fall on the great army. A party of Welsh and English, supported by cavalry, went out to forage and to plunder. From an ambush Bruce and his men suddenly appeared, slew three hundred of the Southerners, and vanished again.

A hungry winter of hardships and dangers spent out of England was not at all to King Edward's mind. Without any fighting he came from Linlithgow to Berwick-on-Tweed, where at least there were always salt herrings—

the chief food of garrisons in these days—to be had for his men, and where Flemish and English boats could keep him supplied with luxuries. He wintered there, and then returned to England.

Hardly had he gone, than Bruce crossed into Northumberland by the lonely Rede Valley. He did not slay men nor burn houses, but his army drove a great booty of cattle in front of them when they rode home, and the people of Northumberland had to own themselves conquered. Two thousand pounds was thankfully paid by them for a six months' truce.

Later on he sacked Durham, while Douglas, marching further afield, sacked Chester. Money flowed into the Bruce's coffers, paid by the people of counties and towns who were glad to purchase peace with him. Berwick, the "key of Scotland," he knew would be useful to him, and on a December night in 1312, when the east wind must have been blowing chill from the grey North Sea, he tried to take it. He had some ladders cleverly made of ropes, with wooden steps, and iron hooks to grip the top of the wall. Two of these were up without the sentries noticing, and Berwick would have been the Bruce's that night, had not a dog—he must have been an English terrier—barked so loud that he roused the garrison.

During the year 1313 three Scottish castles which had been English strongholds were taken by the Scots. By his skill and bravery the Black Douglas took Roxburgh. Edinburgh Castle fell before Randolph, and to a gallant farmer, named Bunnock, fell the honour of taking Linlithgow.

The stories of how these castles fell are three of the finest tales that ever were written, but for them you must go to an old poet named Barbour, or to Sir Walter Scott. There is no room for them in this little book.

Bannockburn

In the spring of 1313, before the heather was purple on the hills, a Scottish army was pressing the English garrison at Stirling. Sir Philip Mowbray was governor of the castle, and with him Edward Bruce, who led the Scots, made a compact. If an English army did not relieve the castle by June 24, 1314, it was to be surrendered to the Scottish king.

When Edward Bruce told his brother of the compact he had made, Bruce shook his head at his rashness. "That was unwisely done," said he. "I never heard of such long warning being given to so mighty a king. England, Ireland, Wales, Aquitaine, and part of Scotland are all ready to fight for him, and what army have we? Indeed we are set in great danger."

"Let Edward bring every man he has," said Edward Bruce; "we will fight them were they more!"

Bruce loved his brother for his bold speech.

"Since the deed is done," said he, "then truly will we fight like men, we and all that love us and the freedom of our country."

In England King Edward busily prepared for the great defeat of the Scots and their king.

He levied men, horses, ships, wines, hay, grain, and provisions of all kinds.

Welsh and Irish chiefs, knights from France and Brittany, and Scots who had not yet learned to love their country, were called on by Edward to come and share in the victory. When, at length, it was fully mustered, his army was said to have been over 100,000, 40,000 of them being cavalry, and 50,000 archers.

There were 3000 horses "barded from counter to tail"—that is, covered with mail, like their masters, so thoroughly that no thrust of spear nor stroke of sword could harm them. It is said that the baggage waggons extended in a line would have reached to sixty miles. They were loaded with every kind of luxury, and so sure was King Edward of the relief of Stirling Castle, and of the pleasant days of picnicking that he and his friends were to have that June in Scotland, that he even brought his tame lion with him.

This gallant host assembled at Berwick, and on a June morning, with armour glinting in the sun and gay banners flying, they marched northward, past the silvery Tweed and the high cliffs by the sea.

On June 23, 1314, the army had reached Falkirk, little more than ten miles from Stirling.

In the Torwood, between Stirling and Falkirk, the Bruce had assembled his forces.

The men of the Border were led by the Black Douglas. Those of Moray were commanded by Randolph. Renfrewshire, Bute, and Ayr were led by gallant young Walter Steward, who afterwards married Bruce's daughter Marjory. Bruce himself commanded the men of Carrick, and Angus Og, a chieftain of the west, led the wild Highlanders of the western isles. Edward Bruce and other skilled generals also held commands, but, in all, the Bruce's army could not have exceeded 20,000. The Bruce had no fear but that every man would fight stoutly and to the death, but it needed a brave general to lead an army against an enemy that outnumbered him by five to one.

But Bruce's generalship had not been learned in the ease of an English court, but in years of hardship, when his head, as well as his sword, had to work hard to save a life which was forfeit. He quickly took in the lie of the land, and waited to make his final plans until he saw what Edward and his splendid battalions meant to do.

There were two ways of advancing from Falkirk to Stirling. Either the English army had to come along the old Roman road, and through the village of St. Ninians, or by the "carse" or plain beside the river Forth, which in those days was broken up by little reedy "lochans." Edward, of course, chose the easier way, and Bruce, who was ready with a plan of campaign for whichever way he might choose, took up his position in the park near Stirling, which had been the hunting-ground of the Scottish kings for many long years. Hills and ridges rose behind the park. To the east lay a marshy piece of land, and in front it was defended by Halbert's Bog and Milton's Bog, and by a tumbling streamlet, called the Bannock. At one point the Bannock winds through a steep-banked gully, where cavalry would find it almost impossible to cross, and the bogs lay on either side of the Roman road by which Edward and his men were advancing.

The only way in which the English troops could come to the attack, therefore, was for them to break up into two columns, one column advancing between the two bogs on a piece of firm ground which formed a sort of bridge, and the other going some distance round to where they could escape from the marshes and attack by coming on through some scrubby undergrowth on the fringe of the Torwood.

These two avenues for the approach of the enemy Bruce honeycombed with holes, a foot wide, and as deep as a man's knee, and hidden by turfs laid lightly over them. On the ground between the holes he scattered caltrops, or iron spikes, for laming the horses which managed to avoid these traps.

At sunrise on June 23rd the Scottish army heard mass and were shriven, for in those days the people of Scotland, and of England too, were Roman Catholics. It was S. John's Eve, a holy day in the Roman Church, and so the army fasted, eating only bread, and drinking water.

When mass was done, the Bruce rode over the field to see that all was ready. He found all as he wished, and had his army drawn up before him in full battle array.

"All you," said he, "who cannot trust yourselves to

hold out until we win all, or to die with honour, now is the time for you to leave me. I wish none to stay with me but those who are ready to stand with me to the end, and to take the grace that God will send."

From every one of those Scottish men came a great shout like the voice of one man speaking—"We will win or die!"

When the Bruce heard this answer, and saw not one man leaving the ranks, his heart was glad.

"Such men in battle will hold their own even with the mightiest foe," thought he.

All the camp-followers, those who drove the baggage-waggons, and others who were not fighting men, he then sent off to encamp on a height behind the Torwood. It has been known ever since then as the Ghillies' (or Servants') Hill.

He then sent off the Black Douglas and Sir Robert Keith on a scouting expedition, to gain news of the movements of the English army. At noon they returned to tell him that the enemy was advancing. It was a mighty host, they said. Their burnished armour shone in the sun; their embroidered standards and banners were waving, and from each knight's spear fluttered his own brightly coloured pennon. It was an army so magnificent that it might have daunted the bravest heart.

"Do not tell this to our men," said the king. "A single word may often give despair, just as a single word can give comfort and courage."

Then he went the round of the camp, speaking to his men so cheerily and so encouragingly that even the most faint-hearted felt brave.

Soon the vanguard of the English army came in sight. The nine miles' march from Falkirk on a hot June day made the English long for rest before meeting the Scots in battle, and so the body of the army encamped in the carse near the river. The vanguard, however, were more eager to fight. There were 800, all "young men and jolly," says the old historian. Led by three gallant knights, 300 of them made for Stirling Castle. So sure were they of themselves, and so scornful of "King Hobbe" and his men, that it must have seemed an easy thing to relieve the castle and wipe out the Scots before they dined.

They skirted the wood at the part where Randolph's division had been posted, and the Bruce anxiously saw them riding on in safety.

"See, Randolph," said the king, " a rose from your chaplet is fallen."

This was the Bruce's way of putting, in the poetic words that he loved, the fact that Randolph had allowed the enemy to pass without hindrance.

To this the only answer Randolph gave was to set spurs to his horse and lead his men in furious charge after the 300 gallant Englishmen. When the English saw their advance, they wheeled round, and with couched spears spurred forward to meet them.

But a bristling hedge of pikes—a thing like a great

hedgehog with its prickles made of steel—met the Eng-lishmen when they came to close quarters with Randolph and his men. The Scots, all on foot, had formed themselves into a square, each man in the front rank having the butt of his pike firmly between his knees. On this bristling mass of steel the English cast themselves like waves that break on a great rock by the sea. One of their leaders, Sir William D'Eyncourt, fell dead at once. The horse of another, Sir Thomas Grey, was pierced by a pike and he was taken prisoner. Horses and men were oppressed by the heat. Steam rose from the horses and mingled with the dust that circled round them in clouds, so that they fought as if in a fog. Growing desperate, the Englishmen threw swords, spears, and maces at those grim Scottish fighters to try and break their square. But the men were ancestors of the men who fought five centuries later at Balaclava.

"Men," cried Sir Colin Campbell in 1854, "you must die where you stand!"

"Ay, ay, Sir Colin, we'll do that," they cheerily replied.

"We will win or die," the Scots had said to the Bruce.

"They thought to die in the melee. Or else to set their country free."

And this the 300 "jolly" young Englishmen learned to their cost.

The Black Douglas, who had seen Randolph go forward to attack a force by which he was so greatly outnumbered, hastened to the king.

"Randolph is in deadly peril, sire," he said, "unless help comes to him soon. With your leave I will speed to his aid."

"Let him win or lose," said the king. "I will not break my ranks for his sake."

But the Black Douglas was obstinate.

"By my faith, I cannot see him beaten when I might help him," he said. "Give me leave to go, for go I must."

"Then go," said the Bruce, and Douglas galloped off.

But as he drew near the place where Scots and English were fighting so desperately, Douglas saw the Englishmen waver. The Douglas was always a perfect knight, and so to his men he called—

"Halt! Randolph has gained the day. Let it not be said that it was through our help that he did it. It were a sin to let him lose any of the honour that he, through hard fighting, has won so gallantly."

When Randolph saw the enemy waver, he pressed them the more sorely. Before that terrible wall of advancing pikes the English broke in disorder, and galloped back to safety, leaving many dead and cruelly wounded men and horses behind.

The Scotsmen took off their basnets and cooled their streaming faces, begrimed with dust and sweat. Of all their company, so we are told, they lost but one yeoman.

"Bravely done," said Bruce to Randolph and his men as they rejoined him. "We ought to praise God for so fair a beginning. I trow that a good ending shall follow it."

He then spoke to his army.

"I do not ask you to follow my will," he said. "Rather I will do as you wish. If it is your will to fight, we shall fight. If you wish to retreat, then so be it."

This he said only to try his men. And again from the Scottish ranks arose a mighty shout—

"To-morrow let us go to battle. We will not fail our king!"

"To-morrow be it, then," said the Bruce, and he gave them orders for battle. "We fight for our lives, our children, and the freedom of our land. Our foes are strong, yet with us is the right."

While what was left of the gallant 300 wearily returned to the main body of the army, the rest of the English vanguard, under the young Earl of Gloucester, rode into the park, where Bruce was reviewing his men.

The king did not wear his full armour. He was mounted on a little, well-mettled grey pony. On his basnet he wore a gold coronal, and he carried his trusty battle-axe in his hand.

A bowshot in front of the English van rode a knight named Sir Henry de Bohun. He was in full armour, and rode a splendid charger. When he saw the golden circlet on the Bruce's head, he knew him to be the king. He put his horse to the gallop, and bore fiercely down upon the grey palfrey. A mighty blow he dealt at the king as he reached his side, but Bruce must have made the pony swerve, for the blow missed him. Rising in his stirrups, the Bruce, with all his force, drove his battle-axe crashing down on De Bohun's head. It cleft the knight's head in two, the axe breaking in that stroke.

Bruce's spearmen hurried forward, but the English hastily retreated. The Bruce's lords blamed him for his rashness, but he, ruefully turning round in his hand the shaft of his broken battle-axe, made no reply.

That night the English army spent in drinking and in revelry. Drunken shouts of "Was-sail!" and " Drinkhail!" reached the Scottish lines.

No sound came from the ranks where Scotsmen fasted, prayed, and thought in silence of the morrow.

When the sun of Midsummer Day rose, it saw the Scots kneeling at mass. After mass they breakfasted, and the king then knighted the Black Douglas, young Walter Steward, and some others. The army then moved out of the wood, and took up the positions that the Bruce had planned. While they were taking their places, the English army appeared.

Their burnished armour glittered like gold in the sun. Their gorgeous banners and standards and gay pennons swung as they marched. To the watchers on the Ghillies' Hill above, the host must have looked like one of the most brilliant flower-beds that one sees in a garden in June.

There was little colour in the Scottish lines, no brilliant heraldry nor splendid armour.

"Will these men fight?" asked King Edward, looking at them in scorn.

"In sooth they will," answered Sir Ingram de Umphraville, one of his knights. He advised the king to feign a retreat, and thus beguile the Scots into breaking their ranks, pursuing them, and thus falling into their hands.

"That I will not do!" said Edward proudly. "Let it never be said that I retired before that rabble."

Almost as he spoke, the Abbot of Inchaffray bore a crucifix along the Scottish lines, and each division knelt and silently prayed as he passed.

"See!" cried Edward. "They kneel for mercy!"

"Yes, but not of you," replied Sir Ingram. "It is God's mercy that they seek. I tell you of a surety these men will win or die."

"So be it," said the king. "We shall soon see."

Then he bade his trumpeters sound the advance.

The English vanguard led the attack, making a dashing cavalry charge on Edward Bruce's division. It was a fierce hand-to-hand fight. Many men on both sides soon lay dead.

Wounded and riderless horses plunged and reared in fierce confusion. The heavy cavalry suffered greatly from the pits the Bruce had made for them, yet they bravely pressed on, protected by the English bowmen, whose arrows fell in a hideous shower, thick and fast as snowflakes, sowing death as they fell. There was a crash of splintered lances, the crash and clang of swords falling on helmets, the terrible cries of men and of horses in dying agony.

To the aid of Edward Bruce's division came Randolph and his men. With spears outthrust they moved slowly forwards, "as they were plunged in the sea" of knights. Their foes were ten to one; the grass grew red and slippery with blood. The English spears, maces, swords, and daggers did terrible work. The arrows smote them in clouds. Yet Randolph and the men of Moray held on their way. No rose dropped from the young earl's chaplet that day.

Douglas and Walter Steward came to Randolph's aid. The men of the Border did ghastly execution with their iron-knobbed staves, made in Jedburgh, but the English received them unflinchingly. Soon the blood stood on the field in pools.

The time had come for Bruce to order his little body of cavalry into action. Sir Robert Keith, with 500 armour-clad horsemen, charged the English archers in the flank, and scattered them in flight.

Now was the chance of the Scottish archers. The hard-pressed Englishmen were battered by arrows, and the archers, getting into close range, drew their knives and hacked and cut and hewed their way through the English ranks.

Hither and thither the battle swayed. Now the Scots seemed to be gaining the day; now the English won some ground.

The Scots, we are told, "fought as if they were in a rage; they laid on as madmen."

The gallant young Earl of Gloucester had his charger killed under him, and was slain ere he could rise from the ground, and the loss of their leader dazed his men.

Between the burn and Halbert's Bog the fight was at its fiercest.

The June sun looked down on riderless horses, galloping at mad pace in dire panic hither and thither, seeking escape, or struggling and floundering helplessly in violent throes in bogs or burn.

Many a brave man—

"Down under foot was lying dead
Where all the field of blood was red."

The Scots, with desperate fury, were shouting *"On them! on them! on them! they fail!"* and the English army, though getting each moment into more hopeless confusion, was still fighting with splendid courage, when, by what people call "an accident," the fate of the day was decided.

The camp-followers and country people on the Ghillies' Hill had heard that cry of *"On them! they fail!"*

No longer could they watch the fight from afar. Rich plunder was within their reach, plenty of fighting was still to be had.

With blankets fastened to pikes and to cut saplings for their banners, they came helter-skelter down the Ghillies'

Hill—15,000 of them, or more—shouting the slogans of the Highland and the Border clans.

The English never doubted but that this was a fresh army, and panic seized them.

The Bruce, marking this, pealed forth his battle-cry.

With fresh courage the Scots pressed onward and broke the English line. The English fell back before them, back, further back, until they resisted no longer, but fled in hopeless rout. Many made for the river Forth, hoping to cross it, and were drowned.

Horsemen and foot were driven into the Bannock, until the burn was so full of the slain that men could cross it dryshod. Only a few brave Englishmen still made a stand, but they were soon slain or taken prisoner. The rabble of the camp had come to plunder and to kill, and from them no Englishman might hope for mercy.

The day was lost for England.

Scotland had gained one of the world's greatest victories.

King Edward had watched the battle from a height above the field. Even now he would not believe that the day was lost. Not a minute too soon, the knights who rode with him seized his bridle-rein and forced him to gallop away. The foremost knights of Edward Bruce's division on foot had charged the height where the king was stationed. Their hands gripped the gorgeous trappings of the royal charger before Edward could make his escape. While his knights defended him, Edward laid about him with his mace. The Scots stabbed his horse, but at once he was mounted on another, and managed to get clear away.

Sir Giles de Argentine, the third best knight on the field that day—a gallant Crusader—rode with his king so far on the way to Stirling Castle. "For me, I am not of custom to fly," he said, " nor shall I do so now. God keep you!"

With that he spurred back to the field, crying "Argentine!' and fell pierced by the Scottish spears.

Edward and his other knights made for Stirling, but Mowbray, the governor, told him that the castle was sure to be taken at once, and that he must go on.

With 500 horsemen he spurred onwards, the Black Douglas following in hot pursuit, with sixty men. On the way, a detachment of eighty English horsemen under Laurence de Abernethy met Douglas. They had meant to come and fight for Edward, but on hearing of England's defeat they joined in pursuit of the king.

It was a terrible chase, that race from Stirling to Berwick. No man of the English dared dismount from his horse, for it meant almost certain death. Every man whose weary horse lagged behind was taken or slain.

At Dunbar the king and seventeen followers found refuge with the Earl of March. The rest of his men were forced to ride on to Berwick. Their fate was nothing to the king so long as he himself was safe. In a little fishing-smack he sailed from Dunbar and reached Berwick in safety.

While his foaming horse galloped southwards, he had vowed a vow to the Virgin Mary to build a house for twenty-four poor and godly students if he got off with his life. He kept his promise, and Oriel College, Oxford, still stands as a memorial of that grim ride to Dunbar, and that royal voyage past the rocks and rugged cliffs of the bleak east coast.

It is not possible to say how many men died on the field of Bannockburn, but an old historian puts the number at 30,000.

Twenty-one English barons and baronets, forty-two knights, and 700 other gentlemen "of coat-armour" were slain. The prisoners were so many and so rich that English gold paid as ransoms made Scotland, for the time, a rich country. Rich, too, was the spoil that Edward and his army left behind. The food waggons were well supplied. There were big siege guns for firing stones, and arms of every kind. Gorgeous clothing, chests of jewels, gold and silver plate, had all been brought by Edward and his luxury-loving knights to the Scottish campaign. Magnificent vestments had also been brought, to be worn by the priests who were to hold a service to celebrate the victory of Edward at Bannockburn. A poem describing the defeat had been written beforehand by a Carmelite friar named Baston who came in Edward's train. He was taken prisoner, and gladly bought his life by revising and altering his poem so as to make it sing the praises of the Scots and their glorious victory.

All Midsummer's Night the brave Sir Marmaduke de Twenge hid in the Torwood. In the morning, when the

Bruce came to look at the field of battle, the knight came out of his hiding-place and knelt before him.

The king greeted him kindly.

"To whom do you yield yourself a prisoner?" he asked.

"To none save your majesty," answered the knight.

"And I receive thee, sir," said the king.

As the Bruce's guest, De Twenge was most hospitably entertained, and was sent back to England without ransom and with a handsome present.

To other knights the Bruce was equally kind, and even the English chroniclers could tell of him nothing that was not courteous, generous, and merciful.

Stirling Castle was delivered up, and its governor, Sir Philip Mowbray, entered the Bruce's service.

The king had come to his own, but it was not until October that, by the exchange of the Earl of Hereford, one of the most powerful of his prisoners, he won back the wife and daughter from whom he had parted nine long years before.

Bruce in Ireland

All seemed now to go well with Robert the Bruce. Soon after Bannockburn, his daughter Marjory married Sir Walter Steward, the gallant young noble who had been knighted on the field. In 1315 she had a baby boy, but Bruce's gladness at the birth of little Robert, who became King Robert II., only lasted a very short time, for the Princess Marjory died soon after her baby was born.

In August 1314 the Douglas and others raided Northumberland, and the poor farmers ruefully watched their crops burning and their cattle being driven away. The English durst not help them. Gladly the people of the northern counties paid large sums to the Scots in order to buy peace.

The only bit of luck that Edward of England had was when John of Lorn, the Bruce's old enemy, took the Isle of Man from the Scots. But he did not hold it long, though all his life he troubled the Bruce by attacks from the sea with his galleys.

In 1315 the Bruces sought to win for themselves another kingdom.

Edward Bruce, who was, it is said, "braver than a leopard," was so strong a man and so powerful a leader that he found Scotland too small for himself and his brother. So, when the Irish of Ulster asked him to come and turn out the English and be their king, to Ireland he went, with many brave nobles in his train.

On May 2, 1316—a year of terrible famine all over Britain—Edward Bruce was crowned King of Ireland. It was a strange kingdom that he ruled over, for the Irish nobles were mostly King Edward's men, and the Irish kernes who owned Edward Bruce as king were almost as savage as the people of Central Africa are to-day. In famine times many of them were cannibals.

Leaving the Black Douglas and Walter Steward to govern Scotland, Robert the Bruce sailed to Ireland to help his brother.

In Ireland he won, and he lost. There was none of the steady flow of victory he had had in his own kingdom, and it was a hard campaign, for horseflesh was the hungry soldiers' chief food.

On a May morning, when the blossoms and flowers of spring were at their best, and the grass of the Emerald Isle at its greenest, Richard of Clare, an Irish knight, gathered together 4000 men to meet the brother kings. In spite of his big army, he feared to meet the Scots in open fight, and so laid an ambush for them in a wood. When the Scots drew near, some of Clare's archers sent their arrows flying out from amongst the leaves of the wood. The Scots would have pressed forward to punish them, but the Bruce, suspecting a trick, kept his men back.

Young Sir Colin Campbell, the Bruce's nephew, saw no reason why the shooters should be allowed to go on making marks of them. He spurred on his horse, and with his spear slew one of two archers who had left the shelter of the wood. The other man ran for it, but first let fly a shaft that brought the young knight's horse dead to the ground.

Up to his nephew galloped the Bruce in great wrath. Scarcely had the rash and disobedient young knight risen to his feet, than the Bruce's truncheon felled him again.

"Ye have broken bidding," he said—been disobedient, that is—"and such disobedience to your general might have put the whole army in deadly peril, and lost us the day."

Wasting and burning and slaying, the Scots marched west to Limerick.

After a halt near there, the troops had fallen in, ready to march on, when the king heard a woman's cry.

"Who is the woman who cries in pain?" he asked.

"It is a poor washerwoman," they told him. "She has just had a baby, and we must leave her behind."

"That we will not do!" said the Bruce. "Here we shall wait until she is able to go on. Certes! there is no man who will not pity a weak woman."

He then ordered a tent to be unpacked for the woman, and other women to be sent to care for her and her baby.

And there, because of their great king's great and tender heart, the Scottish army halted, until a poor washer-woman and her little baby were fit to go on.

In May 1317 Robert the Bruce went home, but until October 1318 Edward Bruce fought on, trying to make Ireland a kingdom such as Scotland had now become.

But though Edward Bruce was as brave as his brother, he was not nearly so wise a general. Nor were the Irish people steadfast and true to their leader as the Scots had been proved to be.

At Dundalk in the north of Ireland, a great force of English and Irish marched against Edward Bruce. His Scottish generals begged him not to meet this army in battle until reinforcements from Scotland reached him.

In great anger King Edward answered them, "Now help me who will, for surely this day fight will I! No man shall say that strength of man shall make me flee!"

Many were the women and children across the sea in Scotland whose tears were shed because of the battle on that autumn day at Dundalk. For as the dead leaves dropped from the trees and strewed the ground, so fell the soldiers of Edward Bruce.

At the first onset King Edward was slain by the sword of a giant Anglo-Irish knight, Sir John de Maupas. They found him at the end of his last battle with the huge body of the giant who, in dying, he had killed, lying across him. His body was hewn in pieces and his limbs were stuck on the walls of Irish towns held by the English.

While sad things were happening in Ireland, in Scotland the Black Douglas was holding his own.

So good a watch-dog was he while the Bruce was away that, after many defeats, the English feared to try their fortunes again near the Cheviots and the Tweed.

A force of 500 sailed up the east coast and landed in Fife.

The Earl of Fife and the King's Sheriff went to meet them, but on seeing their numbers their hearts failed them, and they and their followers went inland in great haste. In their flight they met a body of sixty horsemen, led by William Sinclair, Bishop of Dunkeld.

"Himself was armit jolily. And rode upon a stalwart steed."

Over his armour he wore a bishop's frock. "Where ride ye in such haste?" asked Bishop Sinclair of the Earl and Sheriff.

"The English have landed in such great numbers," said they, "that it is hopeless for us to fight them, and we must flee."

"Fine guardians are you to your country when your king is away!" quoth the angry Bishop. "You should have your gilt spurs cut off, you poor cowards!"

Then to the horsemen who followed, pell-mell, the Earl and the Sheriff, he cried—

"You who love your king and your country, turn smartly now again with me!"

With that he cast off his bishop's robe, and in his

armour, spear in hand, galloped forward. In furious charge he and his men met the English, swiftly routed them, and drove those who escaped in confusion to their ships. Their panic was so complete that one boat was overladen and sunk, and all who were in it were drowned.

When Robert the Bruce heard the tale of Bishop Sinclair of Dunkeld, "He shall be my own bishop!" cried he.

And "The King's own Bishop" he was called until the day of his death. The fighting men of Scotland knew him under a name that they loved still more—that of "The Fechtin' Bishop."

The Heart of Bruce

It was easy for Edward II. to see that he could never be the Bruce's master. And so, where force of arms failed, he thought he might call in another power to his aid.

You remember that when Bruce killed the Red Comyn, the Pope excommunicated him. That is, the Pope said that Bruce had committed a sin so great that he could no longer belong to the Roman Church, and that any one who punished him would be doing a good deed.

Edward now turned to the Pope, and begged him to command Bruce to keep the peace.

This command the Pope at once gave. For two years, he said, no Scot nor Englishman must meet in battle. Those who dared to fight would be cursed by him.

Letters giving this command to Bruce were brought to him from France by two cardinals.

They were addressed to "Robert Bruce, governing in Scotland."

The cardinals did not enjoy their mission. On the Border they were stopped by English reivers, who took their precious papers from them, stole their clothes, and let them go on half-naked to Scotland.

When, at last, they reached the court, the Bruce received them most courteously.

They handed him the letters.

"To Robert Bruce," he read.

Then, very politely, but with a twinkle in his keen blue eyes, he said—

"Amongst my barons who help me to govern Scotland there are several called Robert Bruce. These letters may probably be meant for one of them, and I therefore cannot open them. The only letters I open are those addressed to me, and my title is *King of Scotland.*"

The cardinals tried to make excuses and explanations.

When they had done, the king said, quite affably, "Had you dared to carry letters so addressed to any other king, you might have had a harsher answer."

The cardinals then begged him to keep the two years' truce, as commanded by the Pope. "To that I cannot consent without the consent of my Parliament," said the king, "especially not when my people are daily troubled and harried by the English."

He then graciously bade them farewell, and the cardinals had to go away, their letters undelivered.

A Minorite priest of Berwick was next sent to tell Bruce and all the Scottish priests and bishops that the Pope had proclaimed the truce, and that he must be obeyed. At Old Cambus, not far from Berwick, he found the Bruce with an army, making ready to besiege the town.

"Were the letters he brought addressed to the King of Scotland?" asked the Bruce.

The friar had to own that they were not, and was told he might go about his business.

On his way back to Berwick he was fallen upon by "four ill-favoured ones," who robbed him of his clothes and all else that he had, tore up his letters, and allowed him to go on to the old town by the sea, a naked and miserable friar.

In Berwick the people were near starvation, for the Scots were too near for supplies of food to reach the garrison. The governor was a rude and haughty Englishman, and the burghers had come to hate him.

A burgess of Berwick, named De Spalding, feeling that anything was better for the town than starvation under the harsh rule of an insolent bully, got word to Bruce that he would help him to take it.

One night, when Spalding was on guard, a party of Scots under Douglas and Randolph scaled the walls at a place of which Spalding had told them, and very soon the town of Berwick was in Scottish hands.

With the help of a gallant Flemish sea-rover, named John Crab, who might have been at the head of Woolwich Arsenal or the Elswick Works had he lived now, the Bruce armed it very thoroughly.

Furious at the loss of Berwick, Edward II. came in 1319 with a great army and laid siege to it. With him he had a great movable mine, called a "sow." In this men could be brought safely up to the walls and then spring forth to the attack.

As the sow came near the walls, a stone from a great engine that John Crab himself managed smashed it into pieces.

"The sow has got little pigs!" laughed the Scots, as they shot the English soldiers who were trying to clamber out of the ruins.

The garrison was much outnumbered, but every one fought gallantly. Women and children carried arrows for the bowmen.

It was time to distract Edward's attention from Berwick-on-Tweed.

Off to the north of England rode Randolph and Douglas and their men, burning and plundering as they went.

At Myton, near York, an English archbishop brought an army of 4000 to check them.

But with ease the Scots routed this force, driving it in such confusion before them that many were drowned in the river Swale. So many priests and bishops were present at this defeat, that for ever after it was known as "The Chapter of Myton."

The news of this defeat reached Edward as he besieged Berwick. In terror lest the Scottish light horse might do still greater harm in England if they were not checked, he raised the siege and hastened to the south. The boys and girls who carried arrows for their fathers must have shouted for glee when they saw the banners with the three golden leopards set in red disappearing over the crest of the hill above Tweed-mouth.

In 1320 the Scottish nation drew up a letter which they sent to the Pope.

From its earliest days, they said, Scotland had been a free country. It had enjoyed peace and liberty and the Pope's protection until Edward I., "in the guise of a friend and ally," had invaded and oppressed their land. Their king, Robert the Bruce, had freed them from the tyranny of England, but, said they, "should even he wish us to become thralls to England, we would refuse to obey him. *While there exist a hundred of us, we will never submit to England.*"

To this letter the Pope gave some attention, and the result was a short truce between the two countries.

In March 1322, however, the two nations were again fighting as fiercely as before.

In August of that year Edward marched northward.

The Bruce had no wish to have another Bannockburn. He preferred to starve out the English troops, and let hunger drive them home, without any shedding of blood.

For many miles on the line of march every head of cattle, every sack of corn, everything that the invading army could use for food, was driven or carted out of reach.

To the Archbishop of Canterbury Edward wrote that he "found neither man nor beast." At Tranent, in East Lothian, a foraging party at length came upon one lame cow.

"Certes, it is the dearest beef I ever saw yet," said one of Edward's generals, "for it must have cost £1000 and more."

Storms kept the English ships from landing provisions. The English troops began to suffer from famine and disease.

After three dreary days spent in Edinburgh, waiting for ships which contrary winds drove away from the port of Leith, Edward was forced to beat a retreat.

Before going he sacked Holyrood, and on his way south he revenged himself on the Bruce by sacking and burning the beautiful abbeys of Melrose and Dryburgh. At Melrose he slew a sick monk and two lay brethren, and mortally wounded many monks.

Douglas, who followed in the rear of the retreating army, had a fierce skirmish at Melrose with the English light horse. He defeated them, but had too few men to prevent the holy things of the abbey from being stolen or desecrated and the monks from being slain.

A couple of months later Edward was punished for the mischief he had done. Crossing the Solway, Bruce marched into England, plundering and burning the towns and monasteries he passed on his way.

At Byland Abbey, in Yorkshire, Edward and his army were encamped.

When they heard of the advance of the enemy they took up their places on "a craggy brae," which the Scots must pass ere they came to Byland. When the Scots advanced,

Douglas saw an adventure after his own heart, and got leave to storm the hill, Randolph leaving his own command and going with him as a volunteer.

Up the cliff path dashed the Scots and their two leaders. They were met by great boulders, crashed down from the heights, and by a hot fire of arrows. Yet those who did not fall held on their way until they could come to grips with their foes. Then came a fierce fight, and the Bruce, seeing that his men were greatly out-numbered, sent up a reinforcement of men from Argyll and the Isles. The sturdy clansmen did not keep to any path, but swarmed up the crags as though they were stalking deer in their forests and mountains by the western sea.

Before the attack, the English army "ran before the Scots like hares before greyhounds," writes one of their own historians.

Amongst the prisoners taken by the Douglas were certain French knights. They were brought before the Bruce.

"I well understand," said he, with gracious courtesy, "that chivalry could not permit you to be in England and not break a lance in the cause of the king whose guests you were. As friends I welcome you here."

Free of ransom, and with handsome gifts, he sent them back to France. Instead of the money for their ransom he gave Douglas a grant of lands, held on "The Emerald Charter," sealed by the gift of a magnificent emerald ring.

The Earl of Richmond, who had once used insulting words about him, Bruce treated less gently.

"Wert thou not such a caitiff," said Bruce, "dearly shouldst thou pay for what thou hast said." He seemed to pay fairly dearly in any case, for he lay in prison for many a long day till he bought his freedom for 14,000 marks.

In spring of the next year Randolph was sent on a mission to the Pope at Avignon.

The Pope at last consented to give Bruce his well-won title of King of Scotland, and Bruce, in his turn, consented to a thirteen years' truce with England.

In March 1324 a son was born to Robert the Bruce—David, who was afterwards King of Scotland.

Edward of England saw fading away from him altogether the hope that one day the Plantagenets might reign over Scotland. The Bruce was firm on his throne, and now had a son to succeed him.

A few years later Edward II. was a king no longer. He was deposed, and afterwards barbarously murdered, and his son, Edward III., a boy of fifteen, reigned in his stead.

With the beginning of Edward III.'s reign came the breaking of the truce between England and Scotland.

Randolph and Douglas, with many ill deeds to avenge, marched across the Border, raiding and burning. Against them came the little English king on his first campaign. It was a campaign of failure and disappointment for him.

He burst into tears when he had to go home to his mother, feeling that he had only been mocked at by the Bruce's men.

While Randolph and Douglas fought in England, the

Bruce was in Ireland, leading a campaign which failed through the treachery of the Irish.

But the Bruce's fighting days were very nearly over.

Those hard years, when he was hunted and starved, and through wet and bitter weather had no right place to lay his head, had told even on the iron frame of the King of Scots.

A terrible disease called leprosy came upon him, and his courage now had to be used to bear illness and pain.

But he was never one to think of himself. Even now he was full of plans for the good of the country he loved so much.

He built many strong castles, and he started the navy of which Scotland stood so much in need.

He made his home chiefly at Cardross on the Clyde, and there kept "a great ship," which we should now probably call a yacht, and sailed much round the western coast. Sometimes he would revisit some of the lonely islands and glens where he had hidden from the English. He hawked and hunted and farmed, and in his castle he had a goldsmith's workshop. His royal pet was a lion. Its food cost £6, 13s. 4d. a year, and for its cage he paid £1, 13s. Amongst the old accounts of the Scottish kings we also find one from the Bruce's gardener of Is. 6d. for seeds.

In 1325 the Bruce found time to make careful arrangements for the rebuilding of Melrose Abbey, which the English had destroyed.

In 1327 the Bruce's wife died, and in 1328 the peace

between England and Scotland had a visible seal put upon it by the marriage of Prince David of Scotland—"young Davy," as an old chronicler calls him—with Princess Joanna, King Edward's little sister.

The bridegroom was four and the bride six, and great and gorgeous were the wedding feasts and rejoicings at Berwick-on-Tweed.

The Bruce himself was too ill to come to the wedding, but the prince brought his pretty little bride home with him, and "the king made them fair welcoming," we are told.

"The Treaty of Northampton," which arranged for this marriage, gained every point for which Bruce had striven so long. In the same year the Pope removed his sentence of excommunication, and the King of England no longer wrote of "the rebel, Robert de Brus, lately Earl of Carrick." He was now, in letters from Edward III., "the magnificent Prince Sir Robert, by the grace of God, King of Scots, his dearest friend."

In March 1329 the Bruce paid a last visit to Galloway, the country of his old adventures, and the Black Douglas returned with him to Cardross. The two true friends knew that it must be their last journey together. For so grave had the Bruce's illness become, that, as Froissart tells us, "there was no way with him but death."

In those last weeks of his life, the Bruce set in order his own affairs and those of his kingdom, and arranged in every possible way for the welfare of his son and of his subjects.

When death was drawing near, he called the Black Douglas to him and said to him before all the lords—

"Sir James, my dear friend, ye know well that I have had much ado in my days to uphold and sustain the right of this realm; and when I had most ado I made a solemn vow, the which as yet I have not yet accomplished, whereof I am right sorry."

He went on to say that he had vowed that, once he had made an end of all his wars and brought peace to his kingdom, he would go to fight against the Saracens, "the enemies of Christ."

"To this purpose my heart hath ever intended," he said, "but our Lord would not consent thereto, for I have had so much ado in my days, and now my body cannot go nor achieve that my heart desireth."

Then he directed that on his death his heart should be taken from his body and embalmed, and he asked the Black Douglas, "mine own dear especial friend," that he would take it with him to Palestine, and carry it to the Holy Sepulchre.

"Ah, gentle and noble king," said the Douglas, with a sob that choked his voice, "a hundred times I thank you for the great honour that ye do me. With a glad heart, to the best of my power, will I do what you command, though indeed I am not worthy."

"I thank you, gentle knight, so that ye will promise to do it," said the Bruce.

"By the faith that I owe to God and to the order of knighthood, I will faithfully do it, sire," said Douglas.

"I thank you," again said the Bruce. "Now I can die in peace, for the best and bravest knight in any kingdom will do for me what I cannot do for myself."

On June 7, 1329, when the June mornings must have been making his thoughts go back to Bannockburn, the sufferings which the Bruce had borne so bravely came to an end.

"He was, beyond all living men of his day, a valiant knight," says one of the monks who chronicled the history of Scotland in long ago days.

From Cardross he made his last journey, past "the bonny banks of Loch Lomond," and was buried at Dunfermline, under a beautiful marble tomb made in Paris.

Two centuries later, Reformers wrecked the tomb, and in 1819 his body was found, wrapt in mouldering linen shot with gold, and was buried once again with honour.

The promise of the Black Douglas was one that had to be broken.

The heart, in a silver casket, cunningly enamelled, he bore round his neck by a string of silk and gold.

In February 1330 he set sail with a noble company for the Holy Land.

In Spain he stopped, hearing of a war between the Moors of Granada and the Spanish King of Castile. Feeling that, as a true knight, he could not pass on without drawing his sword for God and the right, against the hated Saracen, he halted there.

> "Now shame it were," cried good Lord James,
> "Shall never be said of me,
> That I and mine have turned aside,
> From the Cross in jeopardie!
> Have down, have down, my merry men all—
> Have down unto the plain; We'll let the Scottish lion loose
> Within the fields of Spain!"

From the Spaniards he and his knights received a royal welcome.

There were few knights in Europe as famous as the good Lord James—most fearless, and yet most gentle of knights.

One famed Spanish warrior, his face scarred with many an old wound, looked with surprise at the Douglas's smooth brown face.

"Ye have been in so many fights," said he; "how comes this miracle, that you have escaped with never a scar?"

"Praise God," said Douglas, "I always had hands to defend my head."

On August 25, 1330, the Spanish army met the Moors in battle.

The advance was sounded, and the Douglas, mistaking it for a general attack, galloped forward with his men in furious charge.

"Allah! Allah! Allah!" came the fierce cry from many Saracen throats.

"A Douglas! a Douglas!" shouted the men of the Border, the chivalry of Bruce's land.

It was a terrible fight. The Scots, with no backing from their Spanish allies, were outnumbered and surrounded by the men who were then the most dangerous fighters on earth.

Even then he might have escaped, but he saw his friend, Sir William St. Clair of Roslin, in danger of his life, and pressed forward to help him. On every side of him were the dark faces of the Saracens; around him his bravest men lay slain.

"Allah! Il! Allah!" triumphantly came the war-cry of the bloodthirsty host.

There was for him, as for the Bruce, "no way but death."

Taking the precious casket from his neck, he cast it before him where the fight was fiercest.

"Pass first in fight, as thou wert wont to do!" he cried. "Douglas will follow thee or die!"

They found him lying dead on the field, where the slain were thickest, with the heart of the king he loved so well sheltered under his body.

In St. Bride's Church of Douglas the faithful knight now lies at rest.

Where the high altar once stood in Melrose Abbey, close to the murmuring Tweed, which no longer divides foe from foe, but friend from friend, rests the heart of the greatest king that Scotland ever knew.